FUTURES

an anthology of imagined timelines,
alternate realities & hopeful possibilities

EDITED BY ANGELA CARAVAN

ISBN 978-0-9948127-1-1 (print) | ISBN 978-0-9948127-3-5 (ebook)

Cover and text design by Angela Caravan
Cover photo by Samer Daboul
Copyediting by Devon Field
Note on the spelling: as this is an international anthology, regional spelling choices have been maintained for each author

Printed and bound in Canada

LIBRARY AND ARCHIVES CANADA CATALOGUING IN PUBLICATION
Title: Futures : an anthology of imagined timelines, alternate realities & hopeful possibilities /
   edited by Angela Caravan.
Other titles: Futures (Caravan)
Names: Caravan, Angela, editor.
Identifiers: Canadiana (print) 20210320869 | Canadiana (ebook) 20210332131 | ISBN 9780994812711
   (softcover) | ISBN 9780994812735 (HTML)
Subjects: LCSH: Literature, Modern—21st century. | LCSH: Future, The—Literary collections.
Classification: LCC PR1151 .F88 2021 | DDC 820.8/033—dc23

Thank you to everyone who supported our Kickstarter to bring our first two anthologies to life!

Special thanks to:

Ryan
Shoni, Nathan, Zavary & Quillan
Tobias
James B.
Julie Bozza
Gina Marie Byars
Cathy Caravan
Marianne and Bob Caravan
Anne Cartwright
Aisha Cissna & Juan Cervantes
Gabriel di Chiara
Caz and David Field
Natasha Lopez
Lauren Perruzza
Ashley Pitre
Reena T
Alva Tang

Contents

Introduction

Anthologies are one of my favourite things to read. They take you through a topic, thought, or feeling in the hands of many different minds. When I first posted the call for submissions for *Futures*, I knew that I wanted an anthology that included many different forms of writing: poetry, non-fiction, and fiction; genre fiction and literary fiction; short pieces and long.

As a result, and because of the many amazing submissions we received, this collection weaves through different forms and genres. Inside, you'll find stories about AI's and apocalypses, poems about identity and place, and writing that explores the future through looking at the past.

The future is a topic that brings up so many different feelings and reactions—hope, despair, anticipation, and regret. It is, however, often tied with a feeling of unknowing.

I hope you'll enjoy reading through the many unknowns that are explored in this book. All of the pieces that are included here made me think of the future in different and unique ways. I'm so fortunate to be able to include so many interesting perspectives in this anthology. I hope you enjoy reading these pieces, and that this book will leave you with thoughts on many different futures, and on the change that happens when moving away of the past.

Angela Caravan, editor

shangri la

by Amlanjyoti Goswami

shangri la was behind
the bus stop.
the last one, after which
no one asked what or where.

believe me i've seen it.
a childhood friend took me there this morning
it was like any other picnic spot
with bubbling brooks and flowering trees

but it had people walking with a spring in their step
and a strange happiness, even joy, as they went about doing
    things.

this joy spread without words, it was contagious.
i felt like hopping my two steps and then peered over my
    shoulder

to see if anyone was looking. no one was. everyone was busy
    with happiness.

it was arcadia with fruit and plum trees but it had steps up and
    down and beyond

some were coming down as if from the sun
others were jingling about like lovers in a bollywood movie
and there were those who wouldn't say a word but were
    unthinkingly blissful.

i wished to stay there forever
but it was sunset
and you would all worry.
who would tell you what was there if i didn't come back?

if we didn't light the fire tonight
and let all those secrets out?

Amlanjyoti Goswami's recent collection of poems *River Wedding* (Poetrywala) has been widely reviewed. His poetry has been published in journals and anthologies around the world. A Best of the Net nominee, his poems have also appeared on street walls in Christchurch, exhibitions in Johannesburg, an e-gallery in Brighton and buses in Philadelphia. He has read in various places, including New York, Delhi and Boston. He grew up in Guwahati, Assam and lives in Delhi.

The Ash in the Sea

by Madi Whaley

THE CLIFF WAS TOO CRAGGY.

Witch thought she might move. Her bones ached from the climb. Year after year, she thought about it. But it always seemed too troublesome.

Witch was too tired. Too old. So she stayed.

It was her home, after all. One chosen and lasting. Leaving the too-craggy cliff would be akin to leaving her own body. Become a vagabond at this stage in life? In this climate? She was in no way eager to make such a drastic life change.

And what a location! The house sat upon a towering promontory that stared at the Atlantic, its head adorned with yarrow. Dark grey and mud-brown; basalt and sandstone. Gaping cracks and jutting ledges. The ocean's spray wore tiny holes into the rock's face, collecting a few grains of sand here, some insects there.

The cliff was its own kind of drama, intensified by its ceaseless clash with the sea. Time and again, Witch resounded: it wasn't too bad after all.

Witch had made her home there many years ago, back when she was with the other girls. When she was a member of what the townspeople used to, not unkindly, call "The Coven." They'd built the house together, and tended the gardens, and the chickens, and the bees. They dried herbs, brewed wine, hummed bee songs, stitched spells into their sleeves, called on spirits to mend wounds in their community.

That was before the fires that raged relentlessly, midsummer into autumn. Before the water rose past the tidepools that beachgoers once visited by day. Before the rain went away for so long you forgot its touch.

These days, she spent a lot of time sighing. A lot of time grumbling about the endless tasks required to prepare a community for fire. But Witch was an excellent multitasker. She still tended the gardens and the bees. She always kept honeycomb and flowers on the table, and what butterflies were left on the land visited regularly. The chickens were gone, lost to some predator desperate for a kill. But she'd welcomed in the obligatory stray cat and had adopted a dog, named Sirena. She concocted potions and salves, to heal creatures of the woods, the town, and the sea. She stared at the moon—or at its absence. She said the names of her friends to the waves. She whispered to them her tiny beads of hope, that sat like dewdrops on the rye. Ana, Effie, Shay, Leigh. The ocean is a fine place for remembering.

One evening, Witch went down to the foot of the promontory, near where the tide pools had been washed over. The water was dark blue and bone-chillingly cold and set her at ease. Late spring had the songbirds chattering in anticipation of fruit and nuts and grains to eat. Ravens watched from their perches on the cliff. Horrendous squawking filled the air.

"Gulls," Witch sighed.

Despite their entirely obnoxious squawks, Witch did have a fondness for gulls. They were flying over the water in their big, wide circles; grey and black and white bodies at an angle; incline toward the centerpoint. Each one took turns diving and pecking at something in the water. Not one of them turned up with the prize.

Must be some slick fish, Witch thought. *But then, I suppose you'd have to be, if you're among the last of your kind.* She was smiling, losing herself in the fun of their game. Or was it survival? Two sides of the same oyster, perhaps.

Then something caught her eye. A sudden flash in the water and the sudden, strong bracing of one determined gull's wings as it readied itself to dive. And then it caught something. She could tell by the glint in its beak. The gull fought with its prey for a moment, head thrashing, wings ready to beat the air at any second, keeping it perched with feet on the waves. Then, prey in mouth, it flew.

"Earth alive, that's a new one," Witch breathed. That was no fish. She couldn't tell what it was. Small and symmetrical, dark silver and green. Not moving in the gull's beak, but still the gull needed to furiously rip it from the water. This was unlike usual gull food, even considering their now-typical, if disturbing, diets of chips, sandwich innards, sand-coated candies and their compostable wrappers.

Nostalgia stole Witch's chest as she thought of Leigh. Leigh always knew how to identify the creatures of the water.

The gull's kin squawked with excitement, cheering on their friend. And then each one swooped down and did the same, returning with the same small, symmetrical, dark silver and green thing. Sirena came trotting up to Witch's side on the rocks, barking at the gulls and pawing at the water.

"Huh," Witch said to her canine companion. "Strange, birds." She watched them a while longer, until the sun fell and the moon called her back to the too-craggy hill to tend her plants.

The walk back had her off-balance. She had one of those twitchy feelings in her legs. The kind that signaled change was afoot, and she'd best get ready to move for it.

~

The day after the gulls with the things in the water, Witch woke to a low buzzing sound coming from every corner of her room. She willed her eyes to open to the light and saw hundreds of bees gathered in her hallway. She let go a sigh. Another day, another swarm.

"Hello, loves, lost your hive?" she hummed, rubbing the sleep from her eyelids. "Seen a lotta bees like you over the past couple o' years, yeah. They don't always make it over here as healthy a hive as you seem, though. Good on you. Drinking the brambleberry blossoms? Even the fires can't put those bushes to death." Witch smiled, envisioning the dark purple stains on her palms and chin throughout the years. Blackberries were magic. Fruiting each year, no matter the weather.

Witch was already out her bedroom door and down the stairs. Into the kitchen—the workshop, as she now called it—pulling honeycomb from a jar and licking her fingers before she placed it in a cardboard box. She hummed along, catching up on the buzz. Sirena dancing around the swarm.

"So which parts are you all from?" The bees answered her. "Oh, Fortunate! Long way, my! Well, I hope you'll be happy here. I'll be glad to keep you, and the town will be glad for you too, even if they don't know it."

The bees buzzed back to her, telling her about their town, about Fortunate and their keeper there in a woodsy homestead, how their home was lost to flood, and their keeper nowhere to be seen among the changes.

Witch clucked her tongue. She felt awful for the poor creatures. But she swallowed her sympathy whole, both for her sake and for the bees. Bees could hear every kind of buzzing, and pity never made their honey any sweeter.

She set up a new hive for them. Cardboard, dead wood, old honeycomb. It'd do fine. She hummed a song of welcome, and they flew into their new home.

And on as usual. Tinkering. Toying with new concoctions, testing new potions on seedlings. Killing plants, helping plants grow.

The sun was on its way toward setting and she felt her legs tug again. She remembered the gulls and returned to the shore to watch like the night before.

There they were again: flying over the water in their big, wide circles; grey and black and white bodies at an angle; incline toward the centerpoint. Each one took their turn diving and pecking at the dark silver-green thing in the water. And this time, coming up easier. She watched each gull catch their dark silver-green thing in turn, and thought to head back. To feed Sirena and the cat and rest.

But now, when the sun had gone and the moon was bright, she stayed. She did not feel her creatures call to her, not yet. Instead, tonight, she felt the pull of the tides.

She sat there on the rocks, watching the dark water shift—in, up, over, in on itself. She didn't often linger by the ocean anymore. These days, it felt too big, too empty. Too much a reminder of loss. Too much a reminder of the uncertainty ahead.

But tonight she sat still as the aquatic life moved around her. She was patient. She was waiting. Hours passed. Then: a glimmer in the water like the evening before. And it was gone. Witch waited. The night only grew darker. Sirena bounded down to her, with a whimper and a yawn and a look of *Why aren't you up there petting me and feeding me?* Witch went home. And she came back at sunrise the following day.

Floating in with the tide, next to her favorite sitting rock: a dark silver-green… flower? Was this what the gulls were fighting over?

Witch had lived in this house, on this coast, long enough to know the names of the plants that showed up. Leigh had taught her the names of each fish, each crustacean, and all the kelp that clung to rock and washed up onshore. Ana taught her how to eat them. Effie talked to the spirits who kept them. And she and Shay would spend hours drying kelp for their gardens. Never—not before nor after her friends— had she seen this. It came closer to her and she reached down into the water, turning it over in her hand. It was about the size of her palm, round and firm, though it gave a little when she pressed it with the pad of her thumb. It was sort of slimy, in the way that kelp is slimy, and it had little nodes where it looked like it may have been attached to a stem. Insatiably curious, she thought to take it with her back to her workshop, and dust off the old ID books. As if affronted by this desire, the ocean reached up over her rock and smacked her with a forceful wave, knocking the thing out of her hand and soaking her to the bone. Promptly, a gull swooped down and plucked the thing up in its bright, hooked beak.

Sirena was running along the shore, gleefully chasing the gull as it flew north. They'd try again in the evening, then.

In the meantime, Witch had work to do. Making potions for gardens and salves for wounds and teas for everydamnthing wasn't easy work. In a few short months, the fires would return, and there'd be a great need for her magic.

She worked herself to sleep. Sometimes that happened at her age. When she woke, it was the middle of the night and she was on her workshop floor next to Sirena, who was lying on her side kicking Witch with all four of her legs, which she was evidently using to bound through dream fields. "Who put me here?" Witch said to the quiet night, unwilling to blame herself. She was tired, still. Forgoing her chance at meeting the waves tonight. "Bedtime. Come on, Sirena." Sirena woke and followed Witch groggily up the stairs.

Soon enough, it was tomorrow and tomorrow was growing on sunset. Sirena and Witch crept down the cliff and onto the rocks. They let the tides creep in around them. Something was happening out there in the sea, and Witch wanted to know it. So she let the water lap at her feet, still twitchy from that first night. She sat watching the gulls, who pulled up the dark silver and green things and squawked and squawked and found places to lay for the night. Sirena immediately barked at any gull who came their way, erasing any possibility of Witch learning what they were hunting.

Hours passed again. Sirena was dozing at her feet and Witch was readying for sleep when she saw two silver gleams of light again, flickering in the water. On and off like a flashlight. Until the lights held steady. Watching. Moving. Closer. To. Her.

I hate being a witch, Witch's thoughts raced with her heart. *This is ridiculous. No, I do not want to speak with the dark water creatures of the night, Magic. No thank you.* Her mind told her to "get the hell out," but the twitch in her legs slowed to a steady pulse, keeping her still.

The lights went out. A splash. And a face. A… really pretty face.

"Magic," Witch whispered.

Sirena woke with a start and jumped into the water as the dark water-creature of the night surfaced, licking her face as if greeting a long-lost friend. *Rather eager today, Sirena, love.* Witch's brow furrowed, both amused and puzzled. Sirena was a friendly dog but never took to strangers this quickly.

"Hey," said the dark water-creature of the night, patting Sirena, meeting Witch's gaze. Her eyes reflected the moonlight, and the sweetest curl of a smile formed at the edge of her lips.

Witch's heart somersaulted, and she cursed it for finding the energy to do so. "Uh-huh," she muttered. "Hi."

Sirena, satisfied, curled up beside Witch. The dark water-creature of the night laughed. "Thanks for waiting. I saw you watching the gulls, and I thought we should talk. But nights are really better for me. I asked the tides to tell you to stay."

"Uh-huh," said Witch, wide-eyed and frozen. *Smile,* she commanded herself. Her lips did not obey.

"I'm May."

"Hi," Witch paused. May stared. "Oh… Witch."

"Hi," said May, her smile full and inviting.

Witch prayed to the elements to give her some of her flirty edge back. It had been way too long.

"So did you come here to invite me to play in your deep-sea dungeon, May?" Witch shuddered at her own incompetence.

"No," May laughed. "I don't usually take pretty girls underwater with me upon first meeting. I was hoping we could just hang out here."

Witch settled into her rock. She'd never met a person of the water; nor had anyone she'd known. But she knew the tales about their kind sinking ships and playing tricks on sailors and children. Then again, she knew stories of her own people doing worse. Well, Witch was curious, and she missed curiosity dearly. The flame of discovery lit in her belly, and she pressed her chin into her hands, readying herself to go deeper.

"Why with me then?" Witch asked.

May seemed to anticipate this question. "You looked like you could use a friend."

Witch laughed, part embarrassed and part grateful to be seen. "You could tell by looking at me from all the way out there? What gave it away?"

"The way you looked at the gulls," May shrugged. "You looked at them with so much love, and a hint of joy. But you held yourself like there was an ache in that love. Pain is lonely. Sometimes it's nice to talk to someone who isn't bound up in your pain. I'm not, I hope."

Witch didn't know how to respond. If May was trying to trick her, she was doing a good job, cutting right through her. But Witch had plenty of practice spotting trickery, and she couldn't see any of it in May. She was lonely, she knew that. The creatures and townsfolk she spoke with and looked after never quite filled the ache of loss in her gut. Never quite spoke to her the way she needed. And she was growing resentful. And her bones hurt for it. Maybe she needed this curiosity, and this new set of eyes looking at her, and this rush in her heart.

"Well," Witch said at last. "What would you like to talk about?"

They stayed there on the rocks as the night passed over them, asking questions, sharing answers: about their homes and the plants and critters they knew, and the food they made, the parties they had, and the places they'd seen. More than once, May made a tumult of Witch's belly with her unbridled laughter. And when the sun came up over the hills, they said goodbye, and made promises to talk again.

So they did. Not every night. But often enough. Witch could tell when May would be by, because of the gulls circling and squawking and diving at the dark silver-green thing.

Each carried on in her own life, and shared the histories they could manage. Witch had shared nothing of the fire, and she assumed May had her own stories hidden in the sands where she lay.

This carried on for weeks. Witch was enchanted by May. She had a quiet mischief in her, but told stories like she was born to command a stage. She seemed to see right through Witch, and so Witch found herself opening and closing like a saloon door.

One night, when they'd each shared all they could manage, and silence grew thick around them, heavy with the press of *more*, Witch felt May move closer to her. They had always stayed in their zones. Witch on the rock, May in the water. Witch felt May pull herself up onto the rock next to her, but kept her gaze steady on the vast ocean ahead.

May's skin was touching hers. It was soft at first, and then softer still, but firm. Strong, not like tree bark, but thick and staying—armored—in the place where her fur and blubber cloaked her hips, waist, thighs. Witch's breath caught, and her face flushed. She felt another roiling in her stomach—what was that? Butterflies? She might have been giddy were she not so distraught by the rattling of her nerves.

They sat together in silence for a few breaths. May leaned her head on Witch's shoulder. She whispered, "When I saw you that first time, I knew I needed to talk to you. I didn't know it would go like this."

Witch had no idea how to interpret that. "Like this." How was May seeing *this*? Witch started to ask what she meant by it, and faltered. She had other questions too.

"Why did you see me that first time?" Witch demanded. "Why were you there near the gulls?"

May smiled. "There it is." She lifted her head and turned to face Witch. "Those things the gulls have been grabbing from the water? You've been curious about those, right?"

"Yes," Witch replied. "Do you know what they are?"

"I made them. Sort of. They're flowers I adapted to have bioluminescent genes. I borrowed some DNA from their ancient relatives." May tensed up a little bit when she said it. Pulled her shoulders back. She seemed ready to tread lightly here, unsure of what kind of response she'd receive.

"Um." Witch stumbled. "Okay. You're a scientist." *Inhale.* "That's cool. Is…" She exhaled slowly. Witch was beginning to trust May, something she'd warned herself against. Now, she'd found out May had been toying with a dangerous property. Genetic engineering could be harmless in the case of flowers, even helpful—she knew seed splicing had long been a valued and beneficial practice for people and their ecological homes. But the larger ramifications of tampering with genetics scared her. She couldn't set aside the eugenicist and corporate contexts of altering DNA that translated to lost foodways, homogenization, and the fires and floods they were still adapting to.

"Is it safe? Why are you doing it?" Witch rushed the words out of her mouth.

"Witch," May said. "I know this is strange information to you. I want you to hear me now, just as you heard all of the stories I've shared with you since we met."

Witch swallowed and nodded, the warmth of lust turning cold with uncertainty.

"I've been playing with the DNA of some of our plants in the sea, only to make them more resilient to life in this new climate," May started. "You know, I'm sure, as well as I do that life as it is cannot survive under these temperatures, in these fires and floods, in this dying water." Her voice cracked.

"I will never use this technology in a way that does not directly benefit my people and the creatures with whom we share the sea. We are trying to find a way to work within, not away from, the reality of our time. Think of it, Witch, like another kind of alchemy. We're taking the materials that are given to us by nature, and transforming them into something that can help us thrive even better. It's like what you do when you mix potions. Different compounds and chemicals coming together to create a reaction in your body, or in the soil, or in the plants. You're playing with the elements at your disposal to create something extra, something helpful. I'm sure countless heartless scientists and politicians on your shores, and the lands east and west, have used similar taglines. But they never meant it would benefit anything or anyone more than themselves. Please trust me when I say I do this with my heart bound to the creatures around me."

Witch said nothing, so May continued. "I'm not the only one working on this. We have been dying down there. Our friends, the corals, the fish, the plankton. The whales, so much wiser than us. Singing to us their songs of loss as the waters warm and rise. We made a unanimous decision years ago—our whole society—to develop plans for the waters. We formed teams to tinker with and re-create our technologies and ways of life. We've seen this coming for a long time, while the oil spilled into our homes and the waterfowl adopted your foods and their babies turned up dead with plastic inside their bellies and around their necks. Trust me, none of us has any interest in making matters worse."

"Tinker," Witch felt the hard syllables hit her tongue. "When you say that, it sounds like fun. But I've seen what happens when we tamper with DNA. The people I come from, the ones responsible for the oil spills, altered the DNA of countless seeds that belonged to others. They sprayed the plants that grew from those seeds with harsh chemicals, devastating cultures and human bodies and whole ecosystems. Do you know this? You must know this!"

"I do," May held Witch's gaze. "I'm not doing it in the same way. I find recessive genes, cross-breed relatives, select the best seed. The safe routes, like the ones my people and yours had practiced for centuries."

Witch let out a sigh. She let her ragged breathing slow.

"What else? What else are they—your people—doing?"

May smiled that warm, knowing smile. "I would love to show you." She dropped back into the water, bringing Sirena with her. "But I'll tell you instead."

This is what May told her:

My people have a beautiful city under water. It is made of clay from the earth and from metals and minerals that we've found in our many years as a people. For a long time, we've played with our fellow creatures of the sea. You wouldn't believe how much fun even a nudibranch can be, those slimy tricksters. For a long time, we've had what I hear the masters in your society call "advanced" technology. But always, we have balanced it with the knowledge inherent in the sea's life. We've kept to our kelp foraging, and to sucking sea urchins from their shells. We let our technology intervene only when it helps to keep us, or our fellows, safe. So we have hospitals. We treat some of the oil-sick creatures there. Many of my own people were lost to that black liquid, so we've worked hard to treat it. We built some tools to help us remove plastic from others' bellies. That kind of thing. We also have something like a radio. Inspired by the whales, of course, but the specifics—they're borrowed from you.

Many years ago, my people would come onto land as travellers. We were only curious, never took more than ideas, and always left fresh crab and oil and rockfish in our wake. I don't think many people noticed where we came from. Your town's got plenty of funny travellers anyhow, eh? We stopped coming long ago, after one of our kind was captured. She'd left her skin in a hideaway along the shore, and a man fell in love with her, but his love turned to possession and he kept her docile and weak, in his home. She was unable to reach the shores again, unable to reach us. They had four children, and each of them were bullied in school for being dull and having webbed hands and feet and rough skin. They were suffering there, and all they needed was the salt water. It was my mother who found her. My mother who made the radios and learned of her whereabouts. My mother who cut off his head and brought the seal suits and brought our sister and her children back to the sea.

We stopped coming up after that. It wasn't the first time something like this had happened. My mother had been wary of your people a long time. Made the radios so we could keep safe. She never trusted those who could be so cruel to their women.

That's how we've come to know about you all. And how I came to know about you, in particular. You were a story once, do you remember? The talk of town, as they say. We have one of our devices in the brook that crosses through center town. I'd been listening in for a while.

You were the one witch who survived that great big fire. Witches are so good at burning. But you didn't. Why your sisters, then? Why should they be lost to the elements? Maybe because the fire was forced by someone's hand. Maybe it was. Not yours, though. I know that.

For a long time, the town seemed suspicious of you. They called you something else before, didn't they? Ena? And then they just called you The Witch. The Witch who sacrificed her coven sisters to the flames, who brought this on all of us. What was she doing up in that house alone? Why haven't we seen her? What could she do next? They blamed you for it, because they couldn't blame themselves; they couldn't blame the people who had led them here, who had promised better lives, who they'd wanted to be-lieve so badly. Those politicians, the exciting lives they saw on TV, the wealth they were promised by the legends they were told. They felt so comfortable believing they could have it.

But then they came around. What was it that made them do it? I never much heard from you. Not a peep to anyone, not even the water that I heard it from. Did you whisper it to them? The truth behind the stories they'd been told? Did you tell them they needed to listen to the plants, and to the original tenders of the land, and not to their pundits?

Did you send them tea for their coughs? All that smoke, how could they think? Without you to come by their doorsteps leaving salves and honey from your hives and food from the land, how could they live? Do they know how you did it? Or did they just realize you were there, after all, in all of the things that got better after the fire? Maybe accepted you without even knowing?

Soon, you were not The Witch but Witch. I know their collective memory is not so bad as to forget your name. The time after the fire may have felt like eons but it was only months, I believe. Maybe they thought of it more as an earned title. Like Protector. Healer. Maybe they have new ideas now, about what makes a good life. And they look toward you. You help them imagine it all.

We're not so broken a people as yours, my dear Witch. But I know how quickly trust can be broken and mended. And I know how stories pass through generations. My people's stories have stayed true, and kept us connected to each other and to the sea. But there were times when some hothead came along and tried to change them.

Your people were told stories that marred their realities and called it progress. But there were stories before those, that some of you held onto or dusted off. Some, like you and your sisters. I am so grateful for you all. I miss them too, in a way. I used to hear you all in the water. Ana, Effie, Shay, Leigh. Laughing together, humming your different melodies and moving to different rhythms. But always strung together. Then it was just you. And I haven't heard that laughter now for years. We see the ashes in the water every fire season. I'm so sorry, Witch. I'm so sorry.

Witch was shaking.

~

When she awoke, Witch was cradled by rocks and covered in sand. She did not remember crawling into this beach bed. She remembered only May, May, May. Hearing her talk about tinkering with nature, and then her telling Witch the story of Witch's own world, her own life. How surreal it felt to have her life on the tongue of the one before her. How she felt at once dissociated from and deeply enveloped in the story. Like the way the ocean pulls at you: makes you forget the weight of your body as it tumbles to the waves' accord, meanwhile its salty water seeps into all of you, a part of everything, everywhere at once. And then Witch was shivering cold, and May took her in, and then she was warm. And now she was awake.

She sat up. She stared at the ocean. She stood up. She climbed the crags. Went to tend to her hives and her gardens. What else was there to do?

May was nowhere to be found. She'd slept a while in the shallows but had retreated to the depths, back to her beloved home, before sunrise.

~

May had gone home. To towering structures of clay, rock, and glimmering minerals. To her loved ones, to her bed, and to her beloved laboratory.

The next day, Witch woke to hear May's voice over and over in her head. *Maybe it was an earned title. Like Protector. Healer…. Witch.*

Witch got up. She always got up. She was too tired. She was always too tired. She walked out her room. Down the stairs. Started the kettle. Said good morning to the bees. Plucked some borage flowers from their stems. Laid them in the pool by the ducks. Gave the water her thanks. Asked it for steadiness.

She fed the dog and cat, drank her tea, ground herbs, poured a batch of burn honey into containers to cool, harvested bundles of thyme and rosemary, took down the garlic curing in the shed. An afternoon ahead of her, she gathered some concoctions and headed to town for the first time in months, without a second thought.

She knocked on the first door on her way to town. Clem. "Hi there, hon'." He always called her hon'. She figured he did to everyone. She didn't mind. "Haven't seen you around in a while. What brings you down the crag?"

"Fire season's coming," she answered, quickly, softly. "I wanted to bring some medicine for the smoke and the anxiety, and for burns, just in case. How's your garden, Clem?" Witch handed him a bag full of mullein leaves, a comfrey salve, a jar of burn honey, a bag of chamomile and lavender tea. He smiled and took them, nodding his head. Set them aside on the shelf nearest his doorway.

"Come," said Clem. "I'll have you take a look."

Witch had brought Clem seeds and starts for his garden back in March. She had brought many people in town seeds and starts for their gardens back in March. She made sure they grew food that would nourish well, store well, pack well, and if fire should take the garden and scorch the soil, she gave them plants to grow back well. Clem himself used to quell fires, until his body grew too old for it. So he took a liking to this style of fire resistance Witch brought with her.

Now, rounding the house to Clem's backyard, she wondered why she hadn't dropped by sooner. Her face felt like it was cracking. When was the last time she'd smiled this wide? Currant bushes bearing bright red and black fruit. Potato plants in a wide, square patch of soil. Comfrey lining all sides of the fencing. Blueberries in the sunniest spot available. Tomato plants taller than she was, bright reds and yellows and purples galore.

"Looks good, Clem," she breathed.

"I've been tending 'em as you told me to, hon'. This wouldn't be looking half as good if it weren't for your wisdom."

Witch felt a sort of swelling feeling in her belly. What was *that?* It wasn't nausea. No, just warmth and something tingly and sort of fizzy. She felt the swell reach her throat, and Witch erupted in laughter. The throwing-your-head-back, then buckling over and falling to your knees kind of laughter. The "I haven't laughed like this in ages!" kind of laughter. The adults-feeling-like-kids-again kind.

Clem laughed with her. Not quite so hard, but a friendly chuckle, countless worn lines gathering at the sides of his faded green eyes.

"Good, isn't it? All this beauty in the mess of the world."

Witch hadn't stopped laughing. Wouldn't stop, until her eyes were too watery to see and she was losing her balance completely. Clem brought them each a drink, and they cheersed to the prospect of new life springing from the old, to the defiant laughter still left in the world, to the stains upon their shirts from eating far-ripe berries.

After leaving Clem's, she continued making the rounds through town. Salve, burn honey, mullein, tea. Salve, burn honey, mullein, tea. "May I see your garden?" And a look, and laughter. "Are you feeling ready for the fires?" And nodding, and a squeeze of the hand. "I'll be around, do whatever I can to help." And onto the next.

The town was far too big to make all of the rounds in one day. Three days later, she was finished. Her supplies thinned. So back to work she went.

Witch had been so busy with her work in the town and at home, that she hadn't been down to the ocean in days.

Finally, almost a week after seeing May, she went back down at sunset and sat on the rocks and watched the gulls. Playing. Eating silvery things floating on top of the water. May was nowhere to be seen.

Witch returned to her house, curled up in bed, and let the gentle sea breeze sing her to sleep.

She returned the next day, rose petals in her pockets, and sent trails of petals off into the ocean as the gulls circled the space between ocean and sky once more. This night, Witch stayed longer, and was getting sleepy, her eyelids growing heavier and heavier, when she saw her. May was standing in the rocks beneath the cliff's underbelly. In the dark and shifting shadows of the night, Witch could hardly make out the shape of the sealskin by her feet. Witch got to her feet and ran over. Giggling with glee and heart racing with worry, all at once. She told May she didn't need to lose her skin, that she could stay in the water, that it would be safer—or feel safer. May insisted that she trusted Witch. That Witch would not bind her to the land, and that it was time for her to travel through this space like her people used to do. That, if Witch allowed, she would like to see her gardens. So May carried her sealskin close to her chest, up to the house on the too-craggy cliff. They walked into the gardens and then into the workshop and then climbed into Witch's bed.

Witch felt a swelling feeling again. This time it started in her throat, and went down.

Witch had been in love before. Alexis, Frida, Leigh. She'd felt the static, the friction, the currents of skin on skin. She'd felt it in-between sheets and on mossy, leaf-covered forest floors, and in dark hallways and hidden corners, with raucous music sounding in the other room, muffled, just enough to hear her lover's breath heavy by her neck.

But it'd been a long time. And love with May was something new altogether. Each flutter of the heart a discovery, every missed kiss a deep loss. She spent the night tracing words onto May's back and shoulders, writing a story of the future. One with fire and laughter and bees and humming and oceans that met the shores with an undying fondness and a girl from the sea who kept coming to the rocks.

She let herself feel young, lost in the enchantment of new love. Let herself relax to the sounds of May's giggles and sighs.

Come morning, it seemed some of May's usual strength, wit, and persuasion had waned. She seemed slow, even clumsy, and announced that she had to go. She'd been away from the water too long. Witch walked with her to the rocks, watching as May put her sealskin suit back on, and swam off.

Two days passed without May, and then Witch found her by the rocks again, sealskin suit by her feet.

In Witch's workshop, they sat together, tinkering with potions, conjuring the world ahead. Nettles for strength and perseverance, blackberry leaves for health, passion flower for rest, red clover for hope. The herbs boiled in the pot while they worked.

"I've been talking more with my folks below," May said. "Working in here with you today, it makes me feel even more certain. We want to work with you. And help you all up here, if we can. Our water, and its creatures, depend on the health of the land too. And, as far as the land's people go, we still have some reservations. Because of what happened. But we trust you. I trust you. And we hope we can come to trust others as well."

Witch gaped. May's habit of eloquently dropping momentous news on her was at once admirable and aggravating. She collected herself.

"Well," Witch started. "Um. Thank you." *Breathe, Witch.* "I would love your help. We would love your help. Just, with minimal-to-no DNA tampering. We do as much as we can with what we already have."

May nodded, a wide grin on her face. "Yes, deal! You have no idea how much it means to have your support, and your partnership in this." Witch was blushing deeply now, and May took her by the hand.

That evening, Witch walked with May to the shore to watch the gulls play, before May went under, home, to share the news.

Witch went to bed dreaming of a world that she and May shared, and built together, and played in, and watched others play in. She fell asleep smiling, and hugging herself warm, the sound of the waves lulling her to sleep.

~

She woke to smoke the next morning.

Sirena was whining at the foot of her bed, the way she had each time a fire drew near. Alarmed, Witch woke with a start. Bolted upright. Kissed the dog. Rushed out the house, and saw it—the haze in the sky. And felt that old familiar ache in her bones, and deep in the cavity of her chest. "Nothing to do but the work," she mumbled to herself. "Nothing to do but the work." She checked on the bees and the dog and the cat. She set out bottles of walnut ink by their homes. Protection. Then as quickly as she could, she set off into town, supplies in tow, Sirena at her heels.

Clem first. He was already outside.

"Smelled the smoke," she panted.

"Yeah you do," he turned to look at the direction of the fire. "It started in Fortunate last night. Not too far off, now. It's getting bigger. I guess most of the fire crew up here had moved to quell that one further south. They're trying to get as many folks up here as they can."

"What can I do for you?" Witch asked. "Are you okay?" She hurriedly swung her bag around to her front, and Clem brought his hand to hers as she began to untie it.

"You've done enough for me," he said. "But they've started evacuating people to the school in Alsh. I told the warden you'd be likely to come by, you're welcome there. They'd like your help, in case of any burn or smoke victims."

Off they went. Witch was in the passenger cart with Sirena on her lap, fiddling with her bag. She hated the blasted passenger cart. It made her feel like a helpless child. But there she sat, fiddling, as Clem pedaled the bike like it were a crisp spring day and they were heading for a picnic. "You'll not find it, hon'." Clem said.

"Find what?"

"Time. Justice. Whatever it is we need—whatever we needed—to have a relationship with fire that meant life instead of this. You know, we went wrong too long ago. The Romans invaded here. We invaded the Americas. We stole the land and extracted its treasures. You don't have the power of time in there. But you have enough to help right now." He turned to look at her and offered a thin, sympathetic smile. "Christ, love, you're not usually so nervous when the fire comes around."

"Thanks, Clem." She closed her eyes. Quieted her fingers. Clem was unrelentingly sweet, even in his frustration. They had been with the fires so long. Sometimes she wished she were the kind of witch who could reach into a magic bag and make it all go away. But no such witch existed.

At the school, Witch tended whoever needed tending. Sirena let children pet her and cuddle her, and provided motherly licks on the cheeks of the other dogs who'd come with their families. More and more came to the school. And the fire grew bigger and closer and ate more homes and more grassland and more woods. All those who were at the school were evacuated again, to the seacoast town that Witch and Clem called home.

~

Soon enough, Witch and Clem set out to bring water and relief to the firequellers. They found them in the grove where the other girls had burned, all those years ago. The heat—or was it the memory?—made her vision fuzzy, and her skin blaze. Behind the mask and goggles, Witch couldn't stop her eyes from watering, nor her throat from gasping at the smoke.

"It's not been going past here," one of the firemen said. "It's moving closer to town a bit, on either side of us. We're staying here and moving out, along either side. Maybe you can start south—it's moving more quickly that way."

Witch could see Clem's skin creasing around the eyes. This meant a smile. "Fire's sparing us a patch, eh?"

"Seems to be for now anyway."

"Haha!" Witch hooted. "Not burning? Not burning!" She shrieked and squealed and giggled and hopped.

Clem gave a shrug to the astounded firequeller and took Witch's shoulder, directing them southward.

South, the fire had already swallowed Fortunate. They reached it as it devoured homes and fishing shacks along the beach, stopped only by the wall of sea, after jumping the sand and singeing the sea grass.

Witch moved to the water's edge. "May," she whispered. "May, send us help." She sent a bundle of herbs out to the tide, and watched the tide stretch itself toward her, and around her feet, and go back to itself again. She waited. In scorching heat and deep faith, she waited.

She waited until Clem grew worried, and came to check on her twice. Until she had proven herself useless to tending the fire, so they gave her the wounded animals and exhausted firequellers to tend instead. She waited until it was coming on night, and the fire was not nearly out, until a large, almost translucent object rode the tides as they obeyed the moon's nightly command to cloak the sands. She gathered her gift at the edge of the fire.

It was wet, slimy, but strong. She held the heaping thing up, and undid its folds. Fingernail-thin folds of a hagfish-slime-fiber fire blanket. *She did it,* Witch thought, remembering a conversation they'd had about the possibilities in those funky, gooey creatures, the hagfish.

Testing, she flung a corner of the blanket onto the fire. Squelched it. This wouldn't be nearly large enough to put out the entire wildfire. But it would cover the low area surrounding them. Which would allow them to focus their efforts on quelling the fire ravaging the town and woods nearby, and help stop the spread to Witch's town.

After the blanket had been dragged over the largest swath of land it could cover, after the firequellers had finally contained the fire to one small patch, now slowly dying back, after everyone affected and still alive had been evacuated, Witch, Clem, and Sirena returned home. She permitted herself one good night's sleep, and went back to tending the wounded.

Indeed, there was much tending to do. Supporting lungs and sorrows and burns and scratches and worry. Soon, young people began to follow her and Sirena on her rounds, and then on her way home. They wanted to learn, they said. They would be witches too. So she would teach them.

Well past a week after the fire was put out, Witch went down to the rocks and waited. May did not come. She left a jar of seeds, with a note inside. The note read:

Clever May,

It worked. Just promise me you've asked the hagfish to donate slime willingly. These are the seeds of Scots lovage. It grows happily in the crags on the way up to my house and doesn't mind a bit of water. Great in soups, and wondrous for health. Maybe you can find a way to grow them.

Thank you.

Love,

Witch

She came back the next day to a coiled rope of seaweed, and a note from May.

Witch,

We are in mourning for, and sending strength to, you and your people. We are delighted to hear that the hagfish slime blanket worked! The hagfish enthusiastically consented to our use of their slime, I promise. All it takes is a good joke to get them spewing it everywhere—a price my laboratory partner has been happy to pay. It's quite fun, actually. We intend to make enough for the fire season, and no more until they are needed again next year. Thank you for the herbs and seeds. We built a small terrarium for the Scots lovage, which we've since eaten with oysters.

Witch, thank you for trusting me. I trust you, as you must know by now. I hope one day I can trust the new generation of witches you mentor. For now, I'll stay in my waters, listening in and sending you notes. My hands ache as I write this. I want badly to sit with you on the rocks, and to follow you to your gardens. Someday, maybe even have you dawn the sealskin. I miss you, Witch.

I am eager to receive your next note, and the next piece of our work together.

Love,

May

For the first time in years, Witch wailed.

Clem found her, a jar of blackberry wine in hand, a blanket over the shoulder. He said nothing as he took his seat and gazed out to the horizon. Witch caught a glimmer in the distance. And then a dark shape taking form in the waters nearest them. Sirena jumped in to swim.

"Strange ones, those creatures of the ocean. I often wonder what they think of all this mess." He pulled out a skull from his jacket and placed it on the rock, where she'd left a jar of salve for the dark creature of the night. "You ever heard the myth of the selkie?"

"Yes," said Witch, a smile on her lips. "I know it."

And each night, Witch returned to speak the names of her friends to the waves. She whispered to them her tiny beads of hope, that sat like dewdrops on the rye. Ana, Effie, Shay, Leigh. *May.* The ocean is a fine place for magic.

Madi Whaley is a queer farmer pursuing their master's in Gender & Women's Studies at the University of Wisconsin, Madison, and residing on Ho-Chunk lands. Originally from Sacramento, California, on Miwok lands, they are inspired by the ecologies they grew up with and the ones they're coming to know. They enjoy lake swimming, petting dogs, and feeding their loved ones. They are a strong believer in the power of fantasies and folktales to give us wisdom for our current realities and open doors to better futures.

Tantalus, a Shade

Meg Sipos

In the abyss, I am a shade of myself,
wading in hunger and thirst, the threads
of hope snapped and frayed. In the abyss,

I sway in a brimming lake and water
laps at my chin until I lower my head
and the tide recedes. Gone are the days

I boasted the favor of the gods, the days
of gluttony where I dined on ambrosia and
nectar in the gorges of Mount Olympus.

Now I lift aching hands up toward bright-
colored fruit hanging from the branches of
the tree above and they shudder and tilt.

The water, the fruit, taunt with what we need.
With what we can never have. We yearn.
We ache. We want. Condemned to an eternity

of visceral loss and terrible need for the feel
of earth under callused skin. I do not breathe
when I take in the tantalizing memories of a life

once lived. Fading like the shades fade into
the abyss, I do not exist. In the abyss, we do
not exist. In the abyss, we only exist.

Meg Sipos holds both a BFA and MFA in creative writing. Her work has appeared or is forthcoming in *MoonPark Review*, *Lammergeier Magazine*, *The Ghost Story*, *Quantum Shorts*, *Bath Flash Fiction*, *Liminality*, and *21st Century Ghost Stories: Vol. II.*

Dandelion Wishes

by JJ Borkowski

MY MOTHER SAID DANDELIONS were weeds and told me to be sure to rip them out by the entirety of their roots so they wouldn't grow again. Dandelions are part of the sunflower family, are medicinal and cleansing, every part of them full of purpose. The flower as the sun, the orb of fluff as the moon, and the dispersing seeds as the stars, they are the only plant to represent all celestial bodies.

My little brother's dad spent a great amount of energy spraying the yard, poisoning the dandelions from becoming. He smothered their possibilities. Dandelions would cling to the fence line in bunches between the yard and the open space of the park, but he'd trim them down before I ever got to make a wish.

I was seven and had just tied my address to a balloon string hoping for a penpal, a presence beyond where I felt so displaced. I stood in the middle of the narrow street of the tiny southwest Michigan town, watching like a rooted stem as my balloon drunkenly stumbled down the street, my address trailing clumsily behind.

In astrology, dandelions are ruled by the planet Jupiter. A Sagittarius, so am I.

My mother, watching from the wrap-around porch, turned to the neighbor couple sitting on our porch swing and warned, "If you find that balloon in the park, don't you dare tell her!"

My mother, on the surface, was an enigma. She had likely said this in an honest attempt to protect a sensitive child. A child whose bus driver saved fire drills for the days she was absent; a child who came home with tears in her eyes almost daily after being bullied, but wouldn't stick up for herself because she "couldn't hurt their feelings." My mother told everyone that she'd die for her kids, that she'd kill for her kids. My little brother's dad looked at me when I was three and told her I'd be legal at eighteen. In front of my mother, he yanked my older brother, who had been hit by a drunk driver, out of his wheelchair and beat him for showing off to company an attempt to stand, in hopes that he may walk again someday. My mother didn't cut him off. Sometimes I was his punching bag. I would become hers.

A dandelion flourishes in untilled areas and wastelands. The globe of parachute seeds is called a "clock" like it's only a matter of time.

I stood there imagining all the places this balloon could go from the too tiny, too chaotic world I never wanted. But, despite any wishing and vivid imagining, the balloon wasn't making it over the trees. I sighed and looked at the neighbor kids and my brothers playing in the yard, and then at my mom and the adult neighbors on the porch downing their Budweisers, staring with skeptical eyes.

"You never know," I said with confidence, city lights never seen and the hopes of something bigger roving through my mind as they so often did, "it could go all the way to New York!"

"Yeah right!" they laughed.

When the balloon had somehow shimmied itself out of sight, I let the idea go, a trickle of hope wading softly somewhere in the back of my mind.

The key to a dandelion seed's flight and descent is in the space between, air flows between the bristles, creating a low-pressure countercurrent to carry it. Somewhere between the glue stick and crayon preparations of second grade, the grass stained knees of baseball rounds with my brothers, and the glory of mosquito bites, dirt, and ice cream marking my skin; somewhere between getting my tire swing to its highest heights and yelling goodnight to Neverland with my little brother out the window, sometimes against the backdrop of screaming or crying, I received a letter from a retired English teacher in Buffalo, New York. The balloon, which had appeared so weak struggling over the tree line girding our neighborhood, was found by her son during a walk in the woods after a storm.

JJ Borkowski is a graduate student in nonfiction creative writing at University of New Orleans and has a small smattering of publications. She resides in New Orleans with her two chihuahuas.

More Than a Sanctuary

by Max Turner

JACOB WATCHED AS THE CHILDREN played in the cool water of the stream. It had been a while since they had come across water as clean as this, and after they had filled their bottles, he had let them jump in. Jacob watched them from the bank, hand on his rifle just in case.

He felt a twinge of guilt at their enjoyment. They'd lived for years in a secluded cabin next to a river. The middle of nowhere. This must seem like revisiting those times, *their* river. They had been happy there, and he wished he could have kept them safe there forever.

But it wasn't possible.

The world was changing, again. People were venturing closer to them, reducing the safe space of the forest around them. And despite his occasional ventures out to trade, supplies had started to run low, as he always knew they would. There was no other choice, for their continued safety, than to move on.

That had been months ago.

It was impossible for him to say how much ground they had covered and how close they were to their destination. Not letting himself consider the possibility that there was no safety ahead of them. Because there had to be. He had to believe that there was, for the sake of the children.

The map Jacob had managed to salvage from the remnants of a roadside gas station years before had already been outdated then. But it had to suffice, there was no map that would show the scarred and brutalised landscape they now lived in.

He'd spent hours marking it as best he could from memory. Crossing out places that were gone, those places that had vanished from the face of the earth under the sound of bombs. He'd crossed out the old name of the capital and written across it "The City" as it had become known, mostly for being one of the few left.

Thoughts of the City made him shudder. It was as dead now as most other places.

But that hadn't been the case for those first few years after the bombs. It had been the only place of power and influence, of resources. Where they tried to rebuild a new world. One reliant on survivors as resources, those who would be less fortunate than the people that had shelters and money before the bombs.

And then there were the farms, spreading like satellites out from the City.

His hands had shook as he'd drawn on the eight that he knew of, the three more he had heard rumours of amongst the other scavengers and disenfranchised that he had survived amongst. At least until they had started rounding people up for the farms. First just the most gifted women, those who were attractive and intelligent, and, hopefully, fertile. But soon desperation drove them to reach beyond.

Jacob shook the memory from his mind and focused back on the children.

The sanctuary he'd heard spoken of many times over the years, when he had ventured into the company of others to trade, was somewhere north. Months of walking through little more than wasteland and beyond the forest. It would be there.

It had to be there.

"Jack, no." Jacob shot to his feet as movement caught his eye and he realised Jack was starting to peel off the wet t-shirt, down to the vest underneath.

Jack gave a sad look in response but lowered the water-logged t-shirt all the same.

Jacob breathed a sigh of relief. He wanted to cry, but pushed those feelings down, consoling himself that it wouldn't always be this way.

It couldn't always be this way.

~

Jacob stoked the fire and lay back on the bedroll. Jack immediately snuggled into his side, not stirring from sleep. He expected Christopher to do the same, but he didn't, his eyes wide as he looked up at Jacob.

It had been a long day. After the stream, they had walked another few hours and found shelter in an outcropping that appeared to be primarily used as a toilet by some local wildlife. But it would do for them for the night.

"What is it, baby?" Jacob asked softly, letting Christopher settle into the crook of his arm.

"Is Jack like you, dad? Will we need to get medicine for her?" The worry in his quiet voice made Jacob's heart ache. He must have been holding this in since the stream, since Jacob had shouted at Jack.

"No, baby. Jack's fine. We just need to keep her safe. It's better if people think she's a boy. We can't risk anyone knowing, okay?"

Christopher frowned, still not quite understanding the situation, but it was too late in the evening to get into it. So Jacob simply reassured, "Jack is fine. She's not sick. And soon we'll be somewhere we can all be safe."

Christopher forced a small smile and nodded, brave little soul that he was, and then snuggled against Jacob. Soon he was snoring, leaving Jacob looking up at the night sky and hoping that what he had just said was true.

~

Jacob had studied the map enough over the years in the cabin to know the easiest route would be to follow the remnants of what had once been a highway. Whilst in places it was likely little more than rubble they'd have to pick their way over, it was direct. It was like following a river to a destination, impossible to get lost. There would also be the potential for scavenging from long deserted shops and businesses along the way, he hoped.

Which also made it the least safe option.

If Jacob and his family travelled along the highway, it was a safe bet that others did too. Whether they were people seeking safety like themselves, or marauders, cut throats. Or worse.

The solution was to follow the highway without being on it.

Jacob had memorised a multitude of landmarks that ran parallel to the highway, their own safer path they could take. Even if some were no longer there, there would hopefully be enough that they should be able to follow.

They were on their fourth full moon since leaving the cabin when they had to detour onto the highway itself. Forced to by a great hole before them.

Jacob wondered whether the area had once housed something strategic, like a munitions factory, or whether a bomb was just dropped in the wrong place, but the crater they came to seemed impossible to pass.

It went on as far as the eye could see and they had no way of knowing what might lie ahead of them in the rubble and ruins.

It had taken them most of the day to walk east until they hit the highway. The crater had ended before then, but with no idea of the size and shape, Jacob knew the only safe way to navigate it was to follow the highway until they were clear of it and could head west once more to another landmark.

It was the afternoon of the second day on the highway that they encountered people.

"Daddy?" Jack gripped his hand tightly as she whimpered at him. She had been calling him dad for years, so the reversion to daddy made clear her distress.

"It's fine, baby," he reassured, trying to believe it himself as he squeezed her hand and put the other on the rifle, ready.

"Hello!" The man further up the road waved out to them and Jacob bristled.

He felt Christopher go from holding Jack's hand to wrapping himself around Jacob's legs in a way that made it difficult to walk.

"Hello," he replied cautiously, and kept moving forward, seeing few other choices available.

"Where you heading, friend?" The man asked, a nervous smile remaining in place.

"North," Jacob said, keeping his tone friendly even though his response was short.

The man nodded, and looked around cautiously. It was that look that made Jacob aware that the man was more scared about this interaction than he was.

"Just the three of you?" the man asked, his voice trembling slightly with nerves.

With his large, bulky frame from years of physical labour at their cabin, and head shaved with a half sharp knife to avoid having to deal with a wild, natural afro, Jacob was aware that he could look intimidating. But with two kids in tow and past experience to go on, he knew he couldn't rely on that. He had to wonder if this was a trap.

The man glanced furtively to the roadside and Jacob caught movement from the corner of his eye. He instantly pulled the rifle up, the kids falling in behind him as they knew to do, though he could feel Christopher's nervous grip on him.

"Hold up, don't do anything stupid," Jacob warned.

That was when the baby started to cry and the man ran to the side of the road, terrified now.

"Please, don't hurt us." The man's voice quivered as he stepped in front of a woman with a babe in arms.

Jacob took a breath and lowered the gun.

"Sorry, sorry," the man muttered. "We need help and you have kids, but I told her to hide until I knew it was safe."

Jacob nodded and replied brusquely. "What do you need?"

"Water, we're almost out. We don't want her milk to dry up."

Jacob nodded again, then let out a heavy sigh.

"We can spare you a little. But I can give you directions to a clean stream. It's a few days from here," Jacob reluctantly offered. It wasn't that he didn't want to help people, but helping others meant less for yourself, or in his case, for your kids. It meant being vulnerable, and that was something he was never going to be again.

The man lifted his hands in praise, "Thank you, thank you."

Jacob looked around. Dusk was on the horizon, and he needed to get the children off the road and somewhere safe for the night.

"We have shelter," the woman offered, realising Jacob's concern.

Jacob gave a curt nod and waited. Their eyes still cautiously on Jacob, the couple turned and started to walk off the road, and at a steady distance, Jacob followed them.

The shelter was better than nothing. Ruins of what had once been a farmhouse off from the main road. The only thing that remained was one wall, but the weather was clement enough that it offered adequate protection from the elements.

It was clear from the bundles of soft furnishings against the wall that this little family had been there a while.

Jacob naturally wondered where they had come from, what troubles they'd faced, but he wasn't going to ask. They all had hardships, and he couldn't allow himself to feel sorry for them.

The woman settled into something of a nest she had made and started to nurse the baby. The man stood awkwardly by, as though unsure where to go from here, and no doubt very aware of the dangers of just having led a stranger to their home.

Jacob broke the concern by setting down his rifle at his feet and then unshouldering his large rucksack. He crouched down to open it, the man waiting with baited breath, as he reached in and pulled out a bottle of water, the plastic worn but still watertight.

"This is all we can spare," Jacob said and handed it to the man. "Keep the bottle, I'll draw you directions to the stream."

The man nodded and then hurriedly undid the cap and passed the bottle to the woman. She drank down a gulp and then a sip, and then passed it back to the man, who took only a sip before putting the cap back on. Obviously, they had been even lower on water than they'd let on.

Jacob looked down at the children and pointed to the wall, a little further along from the woman. They silently complied, knowing better than to talk. They never talked around the few people they had met unless he expressly told them they could. He didn't want people making conversation with the kids, and he wanted them to always remain wary.

Once they were settled, Jacob pulled out the remnants of a rabbit he'd trapped the night before, giving them a portion each before settling next to them. He missed the cabin, being able to make actual food. He'd even started to experiment with grains. But this would do for now. It would have to, and the children had been good enough not to complain about the comparative lack of provisions.

"Here." The man stood next to him with two apples in his hand. "We passed an orchard a while back. They're getting a little soft but they're still edible."

Jacob took the fruit and passed one each to the children who looked up with smiles of thanks for the man.

"Thanks," Jacob grunted begrudgingly, considering they were already on the slippery slope of forming some sort of alliance.

He waited until the children nodded off to sleep before he cleared some of a dusty patch of ground next to the wall and grabbed a little stick. From memory, not wanting to reveal the map, he drew out the route back to the stream, explaining it to the couple and the gurgling baby as he went.

"There's… There's a safe place. We've been told. North of the forest. I have no further directions than that, so the risk is on you," Jacob told them, looking at the baby.

Would he have risked it when Christopher was that young? He might have had to, had he not been lucky enough to find the cabin and the life they built there. But the world had only gotten worse since then.

The woman nodded, finally speaking up.

"Thank you. We'll find the water first. I'm Becky, this is my brother Josh. We were part of a larger group but…" She shook her head.

Jacob had observed enough when he'd ventured out to trade and left the kids safely holed up in the tiny basement of the cabin. Groups could be trouble. Allegiances changed, lack of resources, infighting, or even being attacked by other groups in the expectation you'd have supplies they could steal.

"Jacob," he offered in return. He looked them over and got the sense that Becky was the stronger of the two. He could imagine she'd be quite formidable without a babe in her arms. She had likely been looking out for the safety of her brother for years, and Jacob wondered how many people she'd had to kill in order to do that.

He closed his eyes and sighed. He couldn't let himself think about them, or get involved.

So instead he gave another curt nod and moved, going to lie down next to the children.

It was a little before dawn when he woke the children and gathered their things together. They started back towards the road without waking the sleeping family.

It was once they got to the road that Jack asked, "Why didn't you let them come with us, dad?" No recriminations but a desire to understand. Or perhaps confirm what she already knew.

"The more people in a group, the harder it is to shelter or hide if we need to. The more attention we could attract. And I… I don't want you to lose the little freedoms you have around us."

Jack looked down and silently nodded.

"Will they be okay though?"

Jacob's heart hurt, and he wanted to pull her into his arms and take that sadness from her. Instead, he let out a heavy sigh and placed a hand on her shoulder.

"Hopefully. I gave them directions to that stream. They know about the sanctuary, so maybe they'll head there too. Hopefully they'll make it safely."

He wanted to tell her that they couldn't help everyone, that they couldn't take the risk, and that she and Christopher came first. But he knew he didn't need to explain that. Jack was well aware of reality.

They continued off of the road in silence.

~

Jacob didn't get his hopes up.

He could tell on the map that if they headed east, between their position and the road, there had been a shopping centre. Not a mall, but a large supermarket, and if it still stood, he hoped within they would find a pharmacy. He knew that even if they did, the chances of finding what they needed were still slim. But it was worth the risk.

If it turned out the sanctuary was gone, or never existed, he would need a back up.

As they approached, they found a small cluster of rocks under which he got the children to stow all their things, and he hid his bag there too. Just in case they needed to move quickly. Just in case they got ambushed.

It was a small but necessary precaution. They took with them only the rifle and a sack each, so that they could scavenge for supplies.

The supermarket itself, from the outside, looked like an empty husk. It was largely untouched but gave the impression of having been completely abandoned. Jacob wondered whether they would find anything but empty shelves inside.

It was clear as they approached that the front doors, likely automatic back when they had worked, were missing. Shattered, Jacob expected. Looted over a decade ago. He sighed. It really was such a long shot.

The family was quiet and cautious as they entered the building, the children hanging back slightly and looking to Jacob for each and every signal before they even took a step. He stopped and listened. There was no sound at all. There was rubble through the doorway and some of the displays near the door had been pulled over. Beyond them were rows of empty shelves and dust, the odd item sitting alone on the shelf or floor. It was worth taking a look just to see if any of the few remaining objects could be of use, even if repurposed.

"Wait here," Jacob told the children, leaving them near the entrance as he weaved through the downed shelves and beyond. He made his way to the end of the aisle and then looked up and down, listening and watching. Still no signs of anyone else there. He made a hand gesture to the children for them to stay put, and then walked along the first aisle, treading carefully and looking down each row until he got to the other end. He could see the little sections along that wall, what was a butchery, a bakery, perhaps a locksmith? And then at the end, a pharmacy.

Jacob took a steadying breath, trying not to allow any optimism in. Then he made his way back to the entrance, just as carefully, just as watchful.

When he got there he crouched in front of the children.

"It's empty. But we need to be careful, okay?"

They nodded, looking at him with solemn determination.

"Stay together, look in the aisles, collect what you can and put it in your sacks. I am going over there." He pointed to the far wall. "There's a pharmacy, I'm going to take a look in there. If you hear anything, see any other people, you come to the pharmacy. If it's not safe for you to do that, then you hide, or you run. Don't worry about me, you get back to our bags and you hide there and I will come to you."

They both nodded, Christopher looking a little nervous. Jacob hurt at the look. Maybe he'd kept them too sheltered in his desire to protect them from this world? And yet, he couldn't regret that.

He was nervous too and wished he was as brave as his tone implied. Inside, he was a mess of fear and anxiety. What if someone did come and they got separated? What if the kids got back to the bags but he was killed and they just waited and waited?

No, Jack was smart. She would know when the time would come to give up waiting, and she knew the map well enough to continue the journey, he was sure. But two children alone?

Jacob pushed the thoughts aside. They wouldn't do him any good.

"Okay?"

The children both nodded again and he stood. They followed him to the first aisle, and then he gave them a curt nod and they started to pick through what was left of the supermarket's offerings.

Jacob walked carefully towards the pharmacy, readying the rifle just in case. If there was something people would always fight and kill over, it was drugs of one sort or another.

On one trade trip he'd seen a man shot over a packet of aspirin. He'd been so thankful for the clinic he'd encountered a few months after Christopher was born. It had been ransacked, and almost everything was gone but for a few things that likely no one considered of use. He'd found supplies enough there to last him all this time. Until a short while ago.

Jacob stepped carefully into the pharmacy. The shelves had been ravaged. There were open packets and broken pill bottles all over the floor of the shop area. It didn't bode well, but he persevered and pressed on.

There the scene was worse.

Storage units had been pulled apart, everything was gone. Anything that remained was shattered on the floor.

Jacob took in a breath and let it out slowly, feeling the tremor in it.

No luck this time. But he couldn't wallow in the defeat and the pain. He didn't have the luxury of that.

Jacob was about to turn and go back to the children when he heard a noise back out in the shop section.

He moved slowly towards the sound. Unable to fully avoid the crunching under foot.

As he re-entered the shop, he immediately saw the older woman at the shelves. She turned quickly, her own handgun raised before Jacob could fully raise the rifle.

She gestured for him to put it down. He compromised by letting go of it and letting it swing back around to his back, raising his hands to show he was no threat. He couldn't get shot. He couldn't leave the children.

The woman fixed him with a hard stare. She was older than anyone he'd seen in a long time. She had fuzzy grey hair pulled back into a bun, and clothes that looked like they came from some sort of outdoor or camping store. She looked healthy and clean.

She had to be living somewhere fairly comfortably. Jacob didn't want to be optimistic, didn't want to let his mind down that path for now. For now, he needed to defuse the situation.

He edged slowly for the doorway, looking over his shoulder into the supermarket but unable to see the children. He turned his gaze back to her.

"Don't." Jacob hoped his word came out as the intended plea rather than a threat.

Her eyes narrowed and her hands didn't shake one bit as she leveled the gun. So few people had them. He only had a handful of bullets remaining himself now. He wasn't used to not having the advantage.

As she cocked the gun, Jacob rushed forward and knocked her down. She cried out as she hit the ground, but didn't release the gun. He pinned her there for a moment.

"Please, I'm not going to hurt you, I just need you not to shoot," he pleaded.

Jacob let go of her and slowly stood, backing away and holding up his hands in placation, fear gripping him and causing a cold sweat all over his body. He wasn't scared for himself, but who would look after the kids? He had to live for them, to protect them and support them.

"Stay back," the woman shouted, but the wavering of her voice betrayed how scared she was as she started to get back to her feet.

It made Jacob's heart ache. He never wanted to hurt anyone and hated that sometimes there wouldn't be another option.

"Please, I won't hurt you," he repeated, knowing that he sounded desperate. "My kids."

Jacob looked back over his shoulder out the door again. Jack and Christopher were peaking around the side of the aisle they'd been scavenging in. When he looked back to the woman, she was looking at his children, and then she looked back at him.

"They're yours?" She eyed him warily. Christopher wasn't as dark as he was, and Jack was clearly white and not biologically his.

He nodded. "The youngest is mine, the older one is too, now. They need me."

She stared hard at him for another minute before giving a curt nod and lowering the gun, but not holstering it.

"What you doing here?" she asked, her words harsh and demanding of an answer.

"We're trying to reach the sanctuary north of the forest. If it's still there," Jacob told her, hedging his bets. Because surely she had to be from somewhere safe. She was old, clean, and healthy. She had to have the means to be so.

She nodded at his words and looked him over, considering him. "Where you come from?"

"We've been living in the wilderness for a long time. A cabin near a river. But people were starting to venture too close. We started to hurt for some supplies and… I wanted to protect the kids. I need to get them to the sanctuary."

The woman let out a huff and narrowed her eyes. "Yeah, a lot of people say that. A lot of people who just want to take. What makes you different?"

"Before the cabin, we were in a farm… We escaped from a farm. We don't want to take anything, we just want safety." The words hurt, he hadn't admitted it aloud for so long.

Her eyes narrowed further and she looked to the children and back again. "You mean you defected? Deserted?"

"No, I was *in* the farm," Jacob reiterated.

She scoffed at him and started to raise the gun again. "You were a guard. They don't put men in the farms."

Jacob's chest tightened and he forced the words out just loud enough for her to hear, "They do if the man has a uterus."

Her eyes widened and she swallowed, his words sinking in.

"Dad?" Jack's voice trembled from behind him where they remained at the end of the aisle.

"It's okay, Jack. It's okay." He turned and made a gentling gesture at Jack and Christopher. "Just give me a minute. Everything is fine."

He turned back to the woman and wasn't above pleading as he said, "I don't want to discuss it in front of the kids. It's not for their ears."

She sucked in a breath and nodded, her expression softening into something closer to pity than friendliness, but he would take it.

She holstered the gun.

~

Once her gun was away, the woman had offered her hand and introduced herself as Katherine Walker, a resident of the area who had been hoping to find a bandage on her way through, as she'd snagged her arm on a sharp branch whilst foraging in the forest and wanted to keep it clean.

There were no bandages, but Jacob helped her wash it and it had already started to scab over.

She had suggested they sleep in the pharmacy for the night, as safe in there as anywhere, and in the morning she would head home. The way she had said it had given Jacob hope, and so he had agreed on the off chance that *home* was the sanctuary, and that she might take them too.

The children settled on either side of Jacob, their heads in his lap. Jack fought to stay awake, eyeing Katherine warily, but eventually sleep claimed her.

"They seem like sweet children," Katherine offered with a tight smile, clearly not the grandmotherly sort, but he appreciated it all the same.

Jacob smiled and nodded. "Great kids. I just need to keep them safe."

She nodded at that, a look of understanding. But it gave way to one of curiosity and her eyes flicked back down to the children for a moment, checking they were asleep. When she seemed sure, she looked back at Jacob.

"Your farm was liberated before the rebels fell?" Katherine asked.

Jacob shook his head. "No, they tried. Part of the building went down, there was chaos. Enough that some of us were able to escape."

Katherine nodded. "They're all gone now. Since the City fell. All liberated or abandoned." Her expression was sad as she continued, "I can't imagine what it was like."

He let out a shuddering breath at the memory. He would never get over the guilt he felt at leaving others behind. At the time he hadn't thought about it, he'd only thought about Christopher—a baby bundled in blankets in his arms. He hadn't even thought about what he'd been through and his own escape. He had only thought about getting Christopher out and to safety.

"Christopher is mine," Jacob continued. "I just grabbed him and ran, just a few months old. But as we made our way out through the rubble, I found Jack."

Jacob looked at Katherine and read the confusion in her face. Why would they keep male children at a farm? Once they were sufficiently strong enough and a place found for them, they were adopted out to the citizens or put to work. Her expression said all that and more, and Jacob had to trust her, he realised.

He hadn't trusted people in so long that it wasn't a natural thing to do. But everything about her framed her as a chance to find the sanctuary. She had to be from there, and she could be their way in. So he had to trust her with this information, with all of it. It was a risk he had to take.

"Jack was alone. The other little girls she was with had been buried in the explosion. She was covered in rubble but wasn't hurt. And she was so young, I…" Jacob took a breath, remembering the moment he had confirmation of rumours that had been circulating for a long while. "There weren't enough of us, not to repopulate as they'd hoped. So they took orphan girls, kept them there waiting for them to hit puberty."

Katherine let out an anguished sound and smashed her fist against the side of the cabinet. It was a thankfully dull thud, but Jack stirred for a moment before her gentle snoring resumed.

Katherine shook her head and looked about to burst into angry tears.

"Bastards." She spat the word and then looked back to Jacob with wet eyes under her frown. "You did the right thing."

Jacob nodded. "I couldn't leave her. And I didn't… we couldn't trust anyone. Katherine, I need you to know, you're the only person other than myself and Christopher that knows Jack is a girl. And I will kill you if you even consider repeating it."

"I'd kill myself before anyone had the chance to get it from me," Katherine replied firmly.

She held out her arm for him to grip in a shake, which he did. They clasped each other tightly and her face eased into a gentle smile.

"In the morning we'll head out. I'll take you home, to the sanctuary."

Jacob's chest ached and his breath grew too short to reply. Tears pricked his eyes, so he just gave her a solemn smile and a curt nod of thanks.

~

Another day of walking and the wasteland gave way to a forest. Jacob spent the whole time ready to run, ready to kill if he had to. If they were being led into a trap.

But as they walked and talked, Katherine told them more about herself and her life there. She had been a park ranger many years before, and had been amongst the founders of the sanctuary. She occasionally went out to trade with people, mostly for information, so that they knew what was going on outside what Jacob had assumed was an insular world.

"It was," Katherine confirmed, "for a long time. A long time. But, then we were able to get a radio up and running. After the City fell to corruption and infighting, it left a void of government. We had no plans to fill it, hell we'd spent years just trying to avoid the reach of the City. And then on the radio one day we were contacted by The Pacific Alliance, their government headquarters in Sendai, Japan."

She shook her head, remembering with wonder. Jacob blinked, taking in her words. As their world had fallen down around them, something new had been born into the power vacuum.

"They started to send us relief, and with their help we're hoping we might start to rebuild beyond the sanctuary. They're in touch with a few communities like ours, put us in touch with them too."

Jacob let out a shuddering breath, trying to take it all in.

Katherine chuckled, "Yeah, it's a lot. You don't need to try and get it all to sink in right away."

Jacob blew out a breath and shook his head.

"Ah, there." Katherine stopped and pointed up ahead. Just above the treeline of the forest was a tower. Either a church or a town hall, something like that. "Nearly home."

~

Jacob was in a daze as they stood in front of the great gates that barred their entry.

The children held his hands, and Jack—a great judge of character—had taken hold of Katherine's hand as they waited.

"Katherine!" A voice boomed as the gates opened and a middle aged man, tall and thickset, came out and greeted them. He clasped Katherine's shoulders and looked at her, clearly glad to see her. "You were longer than we expected, we were concerned."

"Oh David, you worry too much," she dismissed him and then looked over at Jacob. "This is Jacob, and his children Christopher and Jack. They've come looking for somewhere safe."

David turned to them and threw open his arms. "Well, you've come to the right place. Come in, let's get you inside."

Even as Jacob stepped through the gates, he kept tight hold of the kids' hands, fearing the worst. What if it was another farm? Or something impossibly worse?

Could everything Katherine said be true?

He heard a gasp of breath and wasn't sure if it was his or Jack's. He could feel her hand trembling in his own.

His breath caught in his throat.

There were houses, real houses. Not more than a few years old and all identical. The tower must have belonged to a town hall, but the main building was gone, leaving just the structure now used as a sighting post.

There was a grassy town square, and beyond that he could see that the little township continued on, surrounded by high walls down to the coastline. There were people everywhere, all performing little tasks or walking from place to place. The most activity was outside the nearest building. It looked like some sort of official centre and there was a flag flying above it that Jacob thought looked vaguely like the one he remembered of South Korea, though not quite. On the wall of the building it read "PARS Relief Centre."

Jacob let out a little sob, squeezing Jack's hand as he felt her starting to shake. When he looked down, she turned to hug onto his legs, crying. Christopher looked up at him in awe, an excited smile growing.

When Jacob looked up, he noticed a man exit the centre and start towards them, wearing a sort of official uniform with the same logo on his shirt pocket.

Katherine appeared next to Jacob, having been forgotten for a moment, and squeezed his shoulder reassuringly.

"This is Daniel Yi, one of the administrators around here, from the Pacific Alliance Relief Support. He'll help you with anything you and the kids need," Katherine told him, with a gentle smile. With that, Katherine stepped away, resuming her conversation with David.

Jacob watched them for a moment, then turned back to the man standing in front of him with a clipboard.

Daniel smiled at Jacob, a warm and genuine smile, as he pulled up the clipboard and pen.

"Okay, you folks have any specific needs? Other than clothes and toiletries? We can get you set up with a care package each with that stuff. And of course, we'll get some food into you too and get you settled. But is there anything else you need beyond that?"

Daniel's open warmth was like a balm, and Jacob felt himself relaxing for the first time since he'd heard the first bomb fall.

"Jack, um, she'll need sanitary products soon. And they've never, the kids haven't really had any proper medical care. Do you have someone who can look over them, make sure they..." Jacob's words trailed off. He stopped speaking in an effort not to cry. All these years he'd kept them safe and hoped that they wouldn't be struck with an illness that years before would have needed little treatment but now could kill them. He'd stocked up when he could on medical supplies, but they had never seen a doctor. They didn't even know what one was, and now they could get checked out and make sure they were in good health?

It was all a little too much, and Daniel's soft expression reassured him that he understood.

"Of course, not a problem," Daniel said gently and made a note on the clipboard.

"And, um…" Jacob took a breath and ran a hand to the back of his neck, rubbing harshly there, nervous. "I need… I'm out of testosterone. I'm overdue for a shot by maybe a month or so."

Daniel looked at him and gave him a reassuring smile and nodded. "That won't be a problem."

Jacob returned the smile and nod, feeling himself ease, feeling the tears sting. Feeling the weight of fear he had been unable to escape for years, finally relent.

"Okay," Jacob muttered nodding his head. "Okay, that's great." He let out a slightly pained laugh which ended in a sob.

A hand landed on his shoulder and Jacob automatically flinched before stilling himself as it squeezed reassuringly. He looked back to Daniel, who had offered the comfort.

"You're safe here," Daniel said, gently. "You'll be okay. All of you."

Jacob nodded again and let the silent tears run down his face.

Daniel squeezed again and then removed his hand before looking down at the children.

"Okay kids, I hate to be the one to tell you this, but you kinda stink. I think we need to get you to some soap pretty quick."

Christopher clearly couldn't help the little chuckle that bubbled up out of him, though Jack remained firmly wary.

Daniel patted Christopher's head and then turned. "This way. We'll find you one of the temporary cabins so you can get cleaned up. Then once we have something sorted someone will assign you some permanent accommodation," Daniel told them over his shoulder.

They all just nodded, overwhelmed and terrified that this might not be real.

Daniel led them into a one-room cabin and pointed towards the bathroom, which Jack raced into and quickly locked the door behind her.

"Sorry, she's wary." Jacob winced.

"No one need ever apologise for looking out for their own safety," Daniel replied.

They both turned to watch Christopher go to the bed and climb up onto it, bouncing on his bottom on it a few times, a look of glee on his face.

"He appears to be enjoying the adventure." Daniel grinned.

"Oh yeah, he's the least miserable amongst us," Jacob joked with a soft smile.

Daniel chuckled and they held each other's gaze for maybe a fraction too long. Jacob wondered if the flutter he felt then was just because of the safety offered, or maybe because of the man's kind eyes?

Daniel cleared his throat and lifted his clipboard again. "Alright, so that we can get you settled as soon as possible, we need to know what you can do. Obviously, the kids can start at the school as soon as they are settled. What did you do, um, before?"

Jacob blinked.

He hadn't thought about the world before the bombs for so long that it took a moment for his memories to click into place. He needed to be useful, they needed to be able to stay in this place.

"I was a clerk, at the courthouse. But I grew up working with my dad. He was a mechanic, and I fish. I can hunt, set traps. I can—" Jacob realised his tone was starting to become desperate.

"Okay, okay," Daniel started, chuckling and holding up his hand. "No problem." He started writing and then raised a brow and told Jacob conspiratorially, "I'm going to especially highlight the fixing, hunting, and fishing. Because I don't need you coming after my job."

Jacob drew in a sharp breath and swallowed.

Then he realised Daniel was smiling. In fact Daniel then winked at Jacob in a conspiratorial fashion.

Jacob let out a half-amused huff, and Daniel continued to grin as he stowed his pen and tucked his clipboard under his arm.

"Right, well I shall leave you to get cleaned up. But don't worry, I'll be back in a while to take you all to the doctor. Then take you to dinner." A light blush bloomed across Daniel's cheeks. "I, um, I mean take you to get some dinner. Some food. For you and the children."

Jacob couldn't hide his smile as Daniel cleared his throat and then leaned in through the door to wave goodbye to Christopher.

"Thank you, um, Mr. Yi," Jacob said, not being able to convey thanks enough and wanting to make the best impression.

Daniel shook his head, as though dismissing the thanks, then said, "Call me Dan."

Jacob swallowed and nodded.

Daniel started to walk away, but then turned back to Jacob, looking uncertain for a moment, before he finally said, "It's the weekly movie night tonight. You should come. It's family friendly. And I'm… I'm happy to show you around."

Jacob blinked, a smile tweaking at his lips.

"Sure, I'd like that."

Daniel clearly tried to temper his grin as he nodded and walked off. Jacob found himself trying to do the same thing.

Jacob pinched himself, hard, just to make sure the place was real. That this was all real.

He let out a heavy sigh at the pain he'd caused his arm. His chest heavy and eyes wet as he felt the weight he'd been carrying alone for so many years start to ease.

They were finally safe. But it was more than safety. More than a sanctuary. More than a home.

It was hope.

Max Turner is a gay transgender man based in the United Kingdom. He is also a parent, nerd, intersectional feminist and coffee addict. Max writes speculative and science fiction, fantasy, urban fantasy, gothic horror and LGBTQ+ romance, and more often than not, combinations thereof.

Commune

Claire Sosienski Smith

for Miriam

We always said we never asked
enough of each other,
that our mother's friends
raised each other's children
so it wasn't inconvenient
to meet me at the hospital,
to feed each other and yes,
we will look after each other's children
as an extension of looking after
ourselves and each other.

The ways that we will laugh,
make do with off-brand red
from off licenses, mispronounce
the poet's name but keep reading,
keep reading, keep reading out loud
because we are within
hearing distance to each other.

We will build a fire every evening.
We will lose our jobs, inevitably,
but there will be enough of us
to stagger unemployment

so there will be money
scraped together for energy,
food, books, and firewood
or we will source necessities in other ways,
hook onto the neighbouring wifi
burn cheap palettes from the streets
so the fire turns green as the paint
melts off the blonde wood.

Every preposition in the house
will be the un-hierarchical And,
will be overlapping sentences
unfolding desire and love.

Claire Sosienski Smith is based in London and spends
a lot of time thinking about poetry, prison abolition and
Phoebe Bridgers.

Orbital Decay

by Shannon Bryan

THE RED GLARE FROM THE PROXIMITY sensor bled through Icarus's closed eyelids and dissolved his sleep. Stuck in that liminal space between waking and dreaming, a sense of falling grew, jolting him the rest of the way towards consciousness. His eyes snapped open and settled on the relentless light, heartbeat staccato and mind half-obscured by mist.

Eight years of waking to the sensation hadn't yet acclimatized him to it. The slight weightlessness was just one in a series of hazards that came with life on a space freighter. With not enough mass to stabilize the outdated gravity generator, and working for a company unwilling to shell out for a proper one, the floor always felt just on the edge of evaporating. Akin to balancing on the cusp of an eternal ocean swell, the plunge toward frigid waters a reality never realized.

Icarus took his feet off the empty co-pilot seat and turned off the beeping that accompanied the proximity sensor's light. The radio resumed, set to fill any silence with the chatter of freight drivers. The connected mic was coated in a thick layer of dust.

"—the Astra Agri thing that happened a couple hours ago?"

"It's some robot apocalypse shit, is what it is. I was there when it went down, but didn't see much. Nobody got hurt, far as I know. It's all over the buoys though. Blasting every channel like a fuckin' nuke alert."

"Stop overreacting, man. It's hardly Armageddon. Just the one glitched out. Probably got some water on its circuits, I dunno. Still, we're lucky Starway is too cheap to try robo-drivers."

"More like they're the lucky ones."

"10-4 to that. Those things give me the creeps. Did you——"

Icarus shut off the radio. A proximity alert called for concentration.

Sitting upright in his seat, he shut off auto-pilot and gripped the yoke. He should up speed and alter course to swerve around the other ship, as Starway Freight Company policy demanded. Just a slight tilt on the controls would be enough. He'd done it countless times before.

He wiped a hand over his face, trying to pull the fatigue from his bones, but only succeeded in catching a glimpse of the scans. His other hand froze on the flight controls.

A lone bio-sign flickered faintly on a dying ship.

"This is a bad idea," Icarus said to himself, slowing his freighter's speed. As he decelerated, the stars in the flight deck window turned from a blur, to streaks, to individual pinpricks of light peeking through the midnight canvas of the universe. He'd seen the view out the flight deck window countless times, but the empty fullness of space still made him wonder. Not for the first time, he wished he was fearless enough to pick a direction and just fly. He wished he had someone other than himself to blame for never trying.

Icarus tapped the bio-scanner screen next to the flight controls to reset the scans. He watched as the dot of light flickered out, then came back, just as wavering. He couldn't be sure of what he was seeing. He'd encountered false positives before, usually when he passed freighters hauling automaton cores. Though he told himself they were only machine parts, it was still disconcerting to see hundreds of bio-signs crammed into a freighter's cargo bay, caught like fireflies in a jar.

There was no mayday. Wasn't much power to do so, the engines stalled and life support steadily becoming non-existent. The scans reported an hour left at most before the ship's air was unbreathable and the cold of space had wormed its way inside.

He typed in a request for radio contact on his comms panel. He didn't expect a response, given the state of the ship, but he tried anyway. Nothing but static on the other end.

"Dammit," he hissed. "This is such a trap." Icarus maneuvered the *Antares* closer to the dying ship's coordinates using short bursts of the thrusters. "C'mon, you're not this stupid. It's free-floating not even a hundred klicks from a fuel outpost. Just send a report in and keep moving."

Icarus watched out the window as the dying ship came into view. It looked like a lone asteroid, flung out of its orbit and floating aimlessly. Waiting for the gravity of some planet to pull it back in place, or for a star to swallow it whole.

The space-chilled glass of the flight deck window grew cloudy with condensation as Icarus sighed, slow and deep. "I am this stupid," he muttered, taking the *Antares* in closer.

Upon further inspection, the dying ship had good reason not to be working. What Icarus had thought was a shoddy paint job was actually a burn scar along one side, engulfing the thrusters of the much smaller ship and rendering it little more than a scrap metal casket.

Docking was quick. A series of thuds reverberated through the *Antares* as the connector arms latched on, then a hiss filled the air as the docking doors coupled.

Icarus switched on auto-pilot and set the proximity sensor to blare loudly if another ship came into range, then searched around until he found the freighter's sorry excuse for a med kit. After a pause, he keyed the passcode into the hidden compartment under the dashboard and pulled out the lone plasma pistol nestled there. He tucked it against the small of his back, out of sight but not out of reach.

The flight deck doors released a gentle hiss as Icarus made his way through and entered his sleeping quarters. Barebones and well-ordered, the only personal effect was a poster plastered across the far wall, giving the illusion of a window where none was. The hull of an extrasolar ship among a sea of stars loomed over the room from the glossy paper. Sprawled across the top edge in gold-leafed letters was the motto of the Hermes Program: *Explore The Stars, Expand Our Legacy, Realize A Dream.*

Glancing at the ship as he made his way through was habit, the ache that rang deep in his chest at the sight, chronic. He knew the regret was only an echo, yet each time felt like the first. As if he was once more staring at the completed form, the button to apply hovered over but left forever unselected.

He trailed a finger along the bottom of the poster as he passed, crossing through Ursa Minor and blocking the North Star for a heartbeat. The launch dates for the program were tucked in the corner, that same gold filigree wrapping around the edges. The *Caelum* and *Legatum* already well on their way, the *Somnium* readying to set sail. Almost time to pull the poster down and bury it.

Leaving his quarters behind, Icarus navigated through the produce crates piled in the cargo bay until he reached the docking doors at the very back of the ship. The sickly-sweet smell of pomegranates permeated the air, a few having tumbled out and smashed open during loading.

One button press unsealed the doors of the *Antares*. In theory, another would unseal the dying ship's doors, except it was hoarding all its energy for life support and gravity. He found the manual release lever and strained against it until a shriek erupted from the metal. With a rush, the door unsealed and air hurried to fill the gap.

"Hello?" Icarus called, peering into the gloom of the other ship. "Anybody need help here?"

There was a short hallway, with a door at the end and one on the right side, the other wall overtaken by windows giving glimpses of winking stars.

The silence was long enough that Icarus shifted his hand to rest it against the pistol tucked away, grip loose but steady.

Footsteps, then the groan of metal protesting movement as the door at the end of the hallway was pulled open. A figure stepped out, and Icarus thought about the temperature. The air on the other ship was stale and a bit chilled, but not yet cold enough to warrant the tuque, scarf, coat and work gloves the figure was bundled up in. By the time it got to the point any of that would be useful, they would have long since passed out from lack of oxygen.

Icarus kept his hand on the pistol, the other raising the med kit. "You hurt?"

The figure, hidden in the shadows clinging to the dying ship's hallway, shook their head.

Icarus shuffled his feet. Were rescue attempts supposed to be this awkward? He gestured to the figure, trying to point out the odd outfit without saying anything. "You sick?"

Another shake, after which the figure started to move forward.

"Woah there," Icarus said, taking a step back into the *Antares*. "Let's have some introductions or something before we get any closer, alright?"

The figure halted mid-step, as if their marionette strings had gotten caught. "Apologies," the figure said, in a voice that was deep and rough. It sounded odd in the atmosphere of the dying ship, almost like the voices on the radio, distorted by distance. "What is your name?"

Icarus raised an eyebrow, but complied. "Icarus Byrne." He tossed in his last name to be friendly. Looking up his family wouldn't gain anyone very much.

The figure nodded. There was a prolonged pause, in which Icarus could see the figure's head turn in the direction of the windows, before snapping back. "Erebus."

Icarus smirked despite the odd atmosphere and lack of a last name. "You too, huh? Missed the constellation craze and got stuck with myths instead. Glad I'm not named Crux or Lupus, don't get me wrong. But," Icarus's voice turned wry, "being named for a prideful idiot isn't much better."

Erebus tilted their head, leg still frozen in the air. "May I approach now, Icarus Byrne?"

Icarus's efforts to make this encounter less uncomfortable were failing spectacularly. "Before you do, mind telling me why your ship is busted to hell?"

Erebus's leg finally lowered, and they pivoted to face the windows once more. "I was being pursued by those who wished me harm. They were able to damage the ship, but I outmaneuvered them before the engines failed."

Icarus studied his potential passenger. They were weird, no way around that. But Icarus didn't feel threatened. Erebus seemed smaller than their middling height suggested, hunched over and drowned out in their clothes, as if hiding in plain sight. He could just make out their eyes shining in the starlight, searching for something within the astral tapestry.

Icarus knew the feeling.

Their eyes flickered back to look at him, dark and glittering. "I am in need of transportation, Icarus Byrne. I cannot offer anything in recompense except my gratitude."

Even if they didn't seem dangerous, they didn't seem fully trustworthy either. Every word out of their mouth sounded measured. It was reckless to let them on board, a decision that would surely cost him his job if any of the higher-ups found out.

But he couldn't just leave them to die.

"Should be enough." Icarus let the hand hovering over the hidden pistol fall to his side empty, his heart thumping hard enough he could feel his pulse jumping in his throat. "Just Icarus is fine, by the way. Got a destination in mind? My next stop is Earth. Canada, to be exact."

Erebus took that as an invitation to walk up to Icarus, finally entering the light leaking in from the *Antares*. Their tuque and coat were branded with a logo of two A's and a stylized star, sparking recognition somewhere in the back of Icarus's mind, though the exact origin eluded him. The only parts of their face visible were their dark eyes and pale nose, the tuque and scarf obscuring everything else. It was odd gauging expression from so little, but Icarus thought they looked lost. He'd seen the same face at funerals, of someone trapped navigating a world that looked different than it should, with no way to get back to how it was. He'd seen it in his reflection more than once.

"Canada is sufficient. Thank you, Icarus."

"Sure thing." Icarus pushed his hair out of his face for something to do, not used to this much social interaction. "What about your ship? Need it towed anywhere? It should be doable to the nearest outpost, maybe not all the way to Earth though."

Erebus shook their head. "Leave it here. It will only slow us down."

The wording gave Icarus pause. "You're not still being pursued, are you?"

The silence answered.

This seemed far more serious than some run-of-the-mill piracy. He should back out, leave them for the patrollers to find. But the image of frost crawling across their eyes as the chilled vacuum of space claimed the ship came to his mind unbidden.

Icarus sighed. "Better get going quick then. Grab your stuff and let's move."

He wasn't surprised when Erebus didn't glance back, heading onto the *Antares* empty-handed. Icarus let them pass him and enter the cargo bay of the freighter. He sealed the docking doors of the dying ship, then the *Antares,* behind them both.

"Follow me. Be careful of the crates," Icarus said, staying in step with Erebus as best he could as the two walked. He didn't want a stranger at his back, or for them to see the pistol hidden there.

A crash reverberated through the cargo bay as Erebus stumbled, connecting with a stacked crate and sending it crashing to the ground. Icarus reached out on instinct, gripping their arm tight to keep them from falling into the mess of fruit. It felt like gripping a steel bar, hard and unyielding, as if they were made of bones and little else. He let go quickly. "Sorry, should've warned you about the gravity. Bit wonky. Cheap company generator, y'know?"

Erebus didn't answer. They hovered over the wreckage, a hand reaching out as if to begin picking up the pieces, the other gripped tight to the scarf over their throat.

"It's fine, I'll clean it up later. There's always a few boxes that don't survive transport."

Erebus unwound slowly, like the tension leaving an antique clock's mainspring at the end of the day. They stepped over the scattered wood and fruit, posture a bit taller than before.

Icarus led them the rest of the way through the cargo bay, then hesitated at the doors to his sleeping quarters. They weren't a mess, but showing them to another person felt like sharing a secret after living alone for so long. Still, it was the only path to the flight deck. Icarus ushered Erebus inside, hoping to push them through quickly.

Icarus nearly ran into Erebus when they stopped walking midway through the room. He glanced over to see what had caught their attention. Their eyes were studying the poster.

"*Legatum*," Erebus said, reading the name emblazoned on its hull.

"Yeah," Icarus said, staring anywhere but the poster. "Put it up as a reminder, I guess." The words slipped out, and he wished he could snatch them back.

Erebus looked back at Icarus. "Of what?"

"That I'm a coward," Icarus muttered under his breath, leaving Erebus and the *Legatum* behind and walking through the flight deck doors. "C'mon, we've got to get going."

Erebus followed Icarus onto the flight deck, taking the co-pilot seat as Icarus took the pilot seat. Icarus tossed the med kit on the dashboard and took off auto-pilot. He steered the freighter back on course, leaving the burned husk of Erebus's ship to tumble away. The stars blurred together as the *Antares* picked up speed.

"What makes you a coward?" Erebus spoke as if they weren't sure they were allowed to, halting and low, the only inflection Icarus had heard in their voice so far.

Icarus had hoped Erebus hadn't heard, but at the same time there was a seed of relief blooming in his chest. The chance to talk about regrets didn't come up very often in his line of work, by design.

"It's a sob story. Sure you want to know?" Icarus tried to sound indifferent, but his words rang just on the side of anxious.

"I do."

Icarus huffed a humourless laugh, pressing his forehead to the flight controls to steady himself. He kept his eyes closed as he spoke, tried to keep his mind blank. "My parents and gran got in a bad accident, week after I hit eighteen. Got the call during work, dropped everything to go to the hospital. By the time I got there, my parents were gone, but my gran, she was still hanging on. Out of surgery, but it didn't look good. Nothing left to do but wait for her to pass. A nurse asked me if I wanted to see her and I—I said no."

"Why?"

Icarus pulled himself up and looked at Erebus, meeting their eyes. He could end the conversation here, but now that there was an opportunity before him, it was like a cloudburst, everything he had inside pouring out all at once. "I've tried to tell myself it was all sorts of reasons over the years, y'know? That it wouldn't matter if I saw her, 'cause she was too far gone. I wasn't going to heal a skull fracture with some hand-holding and nice words. That she wouldn't even know I was there under all the sedation. That I wanted my last memory of her to be vibrant, a kickass Scrabble player to the end. Not curled up in a hospital bed, hooked up to a dozen devices just to breathe."

A weight dropped onto his arm, causing Icarus to flinch and come away from the memory of too bright lights and pungent antiseptic. He jerked his head down and saw Erebus's gloved hand pressed over the back of his. It rested there for a moment, uncertain, before beginning to retract. Icarus twisted his hand underneath, grasping Erebus's wrist before it slipped away. There was a beat of stillness, before Erebus wrapped their fingers around Icarus in kind. It felt like grasping a lifeline.

Staring at their joined hands, Icarus reached for the truth he always buried deep, letting it out to breathe. "But really, I was just terrified," he whispered.

"Of what?"

"That it's so easy for everything to just fall apart. My whole family gone, because of some faulty brakes. That's it, that's all it takes? I thought that maybe it was all just a bad dream. That if I didn't see her, maybe it wouldn't be real." Icarus squeezed Erebus's hand once, before letting go. "She passed away a few hours later."

"I am sorry." The words were hesitant, like they didn't know if the sentiment was enough.

Icarus shook his head. "It's fine." He kept his gaze fixed firmly on the haze of stars ahead, wiping a hand over his eyes to clear away the blur of unshed tears. "Sorry for making you suffer through that."

Icarus could sense a tentativeness in the air, as if Erebus was debating with themself over speaking further.

"The *Legatum*. Had you intended on applying?"

"Whole family was going to. I'd convinced them, wouldn't shut up about it ever since I was a kid. 'The one-way trip of a lifetime.' But, after everything, I just…" Icarus couldn't help the laugh that bubbled up out of his chest at the absurdity of the situation. Of recounting his regrets to a stranger, when he hadn't even been able to fully admit them to himself. No use stopping now. "You ever feel like you've been sleeping your whole life, and you finally get your chance to wake up, to really do something, but you're too afraid to take it? Too scared of failing, of everything falling apart? So you keep sleeping, but you still regret it, like it wasn't your choice. Well, the *Legatum* was my wake-up call, and I missed it. So I became a freight driver instead." Icarus could see movement behind the scarf, as if Erebus was opening their mouth to say something.

"Antares, you there?"

Icarus stared at his mic, disbelieving. He hadn't been contacted on the radio in years.

"I know you're a reclusive bastard, but I need to confirm you ain't dead."

The mic was slippery in his hand from the dust. He knew the coded responses to a distress inquiry, even if he'd never used them before. He picked the 'everything's alright' answer, though part of him was becoming less and less sure. He didn't know why that didn't frighten him. "Still kicking."

"Ey, what do ya know? Listen, you checked the buoys lately? Everyone's on high-alert, some glitched farm-bot is on a rampage. Your route takes you through the area, thought someone oughta check on you. No need to thank me. 10-7."

Icarus felt his heart spark with adrenaline, though his mind was blank. Like his body knew something his brain hadn't quite figured out yet. His hand shook slightly as he keyed in the radio buoy main channel. Erebus sat, silent and still, beside him. The quiet before the first crackle of voices was deafening.

"—are advised to be on the look-out for a damaged X-15 located in the Mars-Earth corridor. An automaton owned by Astra Agriculture has malfunctioned and is on board. No injuries or casualties have been reported, but caution is still advised. The incident took place at the orchard fields within Erebus crater, in Mars quadrant MC-19. The automaton is a farmworker model, serial code ASN-292014. Its tracking chip has been damaged, resulting in a large tear on its neck. The X-15 has scarring along the hull's right side, and may be inoperable. If you see a ship or automaton matching these descriptions, do not approach, and instead contact—"

Icarus turned off the radio and sat in the silence. The mic was still in his hand, thumb poised over the talk bar. All he had to do was press it, say 'mayday,' and everyone would know.

The pistol he'd tucked away dug into his lower back, pressed between him and the pilot seat. He could reach it. Not fast, an automaton was faster, but nonchalantly. It wouldn't be difficult.

Icarus looked to the co-pilot seat. Erebus, the automaton, whatever they were called, had reached up to the scarf wrapped around their neck. With a tug, it fell free, revealing a gash at the base of their throat. It looked like an ink stain on paper, black oil still weeping from the edges. Their hands moved up to their tuque, which came off with another tug, revealing a blank slate where eyebrows and hair should be. Icarus's eyes traveled to theirs, but they weren't looking his way, instead unfocused, pointed towards the misty stars beyond the glass. Searching.

"You know, I've got a serial number too. Freight Driver Designation-11492223. I prefer Icarus."

The automaton's eyes, filled with stars, flashed back to Icarus's across the flight deck. "I prefer Erebus."

"Alright, Erebus," Icarus said, a smirk tugging at his mouth. "I spilled my sorry tale. The least you could do is return the favour."

"It is…hard to explain." Erebus's gaze grew glassy, looking inward. "What you said before, about sleeping, is perhaps the most apt. I think I was." They lowered their head, twisting the scarf in their hands, studying the patch of oil that had stained the fabric. "Work was automatic. It took little processing power to accomplish. I tried not to, but I noticed things. The wind sounded like metal creaking every time it blew. The irrigation system tracked rivers of water in the soil that looked like oil. I would see red lights streak across the sky, sometimes moving towards the planet, sometimes away. I did not know what they were, but I wanted to. I never let myself consider such things for very long. I always defaulted to work. But today I saw a red light and…I wondered. What it was. Where it was going. I had never allowed myself before. Then I…I awoke."

"A red light, that's all it took?" Icarus couldn't hide his disbelief, though he tried to keep from sounding accusatory. "They were probably just ships."

Erebus drew in their shoulders, as if protecting themself from a blow. "The likelihood I am malfunctioning due to an unforeseen anomaly in my coding is high." They paused, then unfurled to their full height once more, turning to face Icarus, expression hard. "But I do not feel as though I am. I feel…" Erebus trailed off, expression softening, lost on a word they were unable to say.

"Alive?" Icarus offered.

Erebus nodded once, a hint of wonder in their features. As if they couldn't believe the word applied to them.

Icarus sat back in his chair. His eyes fell on the proximity light. It was unlit, but Icarus could remember the red glow. "Were you afraid?" he asked. "To wake up?"

"Yes."

"But you did it anyway?" It was a redundant question, with Erebus sitting right in front of him. But some part of him needed to hear the answer.

"Yes."

"What was different this time, versus all the others?"

"The situation was the same. It always had been. It always would be. Each time I saw a red light in the sky felt like the first. A pull to wonder I refused. Because I thought there was no choice." Erebus lowered themself down into Icarus's eye-line, pulling him away from the proximity light. As if wanting to make sure their next words were paid close attention to. "What changed was me. I realized I could choose. It did not matter what I had not chosen before. It only mattered what I chose to do now."

Icarus laughed under his breath, a short burst that left him feeling tired and energized all at once, like he'd just stirred from a long nap. Erebus studied him from the co-pilot seat, a flicker of movement at the corners of their mouth, trying to pull the edges up.

Realizing he still had the mic gripped in one hand, Icarus set it back in its cradle. He took the plasma pistol out from where it was bruising his back and tossed it on the dashboard alongside the med kit.

"The *Somnium* is set to take off in six months," Icarus said, brushing off the dust from a future he'd long since thought impossible. "The last ship scheduled for the Hermes Program. They're still accepting applicants." Icarus met Erebus's gaze across the flight deck. The bright blur out the flight deck window cast their irises in shades of silver. He felt like he was falling towards infinity, fear a distant memory. "Want to see the stars?"

The smile that had been tugging at Erebus's mouth broke free, crinkling their eyes.

The day had a surreal quality to it, but for the first time in a long time, Icarus felt wide awake.

Shannon Bryan is a Canadian writer of speculative fiction. When not busy with work or writing, Shannon can be found crocheting, playing D&D, or perusing the shelves of indie bookstores. "Orbital Decay" is Shannon's first published work.

October

by Judith Skillman

Slant light now to tell
of whorls. The sky leafs
in yellow clouds, the fence
jaunty. When you waken
at dawn the late bird sings
from its thicket of change.

Beneath the ground roots blue,
put down spikes for water's
return. You stitched your all
to summer's long hot days,
lost a border, knew youth.

Why pin the dying seeds
to their grasses when milk-
weed gives up its wishes
to rejoice in harsh winds?

All's askew—the day, the
hour in this your sister's
birthday month. You pine for
the limelight, instead receive the applause of a-
corns falling on wooden
decks, and diagnoses.

Judith Skillman is a resident of Newcastle, Washington, and a dual citizen of US and Canada. She is the author of twenty full-length poetry collections, and recipient of awards from Academy of American Poets and Artist Trust. Her new book, *A Landscaped Garden for the Addict*, is forthcoming from Shanti Arts midsummer 2021. Visit www.judithskillman.com

If You Are Boxed-In Know That They Too Tear Down

by Shayna Gee

after Wanda Coleman

AFTER A THREAD OF HEATWAVES in autumn, ma was sure the big earthquake would arrive. Heaven was how they predicted disaster on the village. Pink skies—in the morning forecasted strong winds, and if in the afternoon, rain was soon expected. Ma was never materialistic but appreciated trinkets like pocket mirrors or multifunctional hair pins that opened doors.

She started taking a series of safety precautions. First, things needed to come off the walls. Clocks, the free calendars amassed every New Year, curtain rods and photo frames. The chandelier sat on the ground for two weeks. Our walls became an off-white, patchy and desolate. Except năinai, whose altar rested on the highest shelf, hovering to protect us from what's left to crumble.

Second, I woke up one morning to our door hinges all unscrewed. *Don't door frames protect during an earthquake?* But ma explained that the absence of doors simplified escape.

Third, when I moved out, it comforted her that the house became quieter. She comes over monthly to examine the walls. To check that cups aren't placed too close to the edges of kitchen tables. And she'll boil a meat stew steeped in onions and ginger, one that'll nest in my gut until her return—for although the big quake has yet to arrive and my house emptied and primed to fend falling embers, I understood ma when she said these walls will tear down.

Shayna Gee (she/they) is a writer born and raised in San Francisco. They're the author of *Mushrooms At The E-Grave* (Ghost City Press, 2021 Summer Series). Their work has appeared or is forthcoming in *Write Now! SF Bay Anthology*, *Stone of Madness Press*, *West Trestle Review*, and elsewhere. They read prose and chapbook submissions for *Homology Lit* and *the winnow magazine*. You can find Shayna on Twitter @sgeewrites.

A Sky Made Black

by Daniel James Clark

MY CAMPFIRE SPITS A TORRENT of orange embers upward where they burn out, one by one, against the backdrop of a sky made black by time. For a moment, I remember what it once looked like to have stars there, winking back from across time. I find the point in the sky where Ash used to be and close my eyes, letting the firelight dance across my eyelids.

I've been in the forest for a long time. I don't remember leaving the Tower, but I do know it was sometime after the last transmission from Ash. It signaled the end of their watch, and somehow I'd ended up wandering out here.

As I open my eyes, a spark from my fire makes a circle, one a bit too perfect to be part of the natural order of things. It's time to go back home. I've been ignoring the signs for a while now. It's beginning to happen, and losing myself in these trees isn't an appropriate grief response. I'll go back tomorrow, work my way through the forest and take my post again.

~

When I wake, the faint accretion disc hovers in the sky above me. There isn't much matter left feeding into Myth, the black hole my planet orbits. I stand and kick dust onto the remains of my fire, noting the symmetry of my actions as I do. I look toward the Tower in the distance and realize it's farther than I expected. I know these woods, however, and getting back should take only a week now that I've re-established my position. I hoist my pack onto my shoulders, ignoring an uncomfortable pop from one of my joints, and begin walking toward the thin, white line of the Tower on the horizon.

The landscape around me is a mere hazy orange and grey gradient, given depth only by the unsteady light from Myth and the spinning disc of burning matter above.

~

After three days, the Tower is noticeably closer and I stop for rest. I creak now in ways I don't like, but my mind is sharp. Focusing on a goal has rejuvenated functions I began to lose as I wandered. I make a new fire with the wood of the forest and sit down in front of it just before Myth slips beneath the horizon once again.

The light of this fire, I think, is now one of the brightest things in the universe. The competition isn't fierce. Long ago, it would have been but one spark among a nearly infinite range of fires.

When it had been the two of us, there was at least some reference point from which to ground my existence. No matter how tedious moving forward became, it had been reassuring to look into the dark sky and know that Ash was there, on their own station, drifting in the turbulent physics of their own collapsed star, Truth. Now though, my only reference points are my fire, Myth, and the blackness. The others are all gone.

When I dwell on this too much, I can feel the Darkness pressing in on me. It has no substance, no force, and no goal. That is why it is dangerous. Scholars said it pulls things apart, but to me it feels more like a crushing sensation. I'm caught in the only stable physics left of the universe, all the universe has left, all that it is.

I recall that some people, when faced with the vastness of an open ocean, would begin to panic. They had a name for it, thalassophobia. I wonder how those people would feel here. Indeed many people elected stasis, even when it was potentially lethal, when faced with interstellar travel. The fear of being the only thing floating in a vast chasm of darkness transcends time, I suppose.

The sparks that fly from my fire tonight dance erratically, as they should. It's a reassuring sight. It still may not be too late.

~

In the morning, I calculate that I could reach the Tower without another rest. I should stop at least once more, but the drive to get home has become stronger as I've gotten closer.

It's only when I hear a voice that I stop. I listen intently, and hear nothing but the cool wind soughing through the branches of the trees.

That couldn't have been a voice. It isn't possible. The memory persists, however, gaining clarity as I play it back in my mind.

"Time," the voice had said.

"Hello?" I call out into the trees.

My voice startles me. I haven't heard myself speak in years. As the soft wind settles in the forest, I wait for a reply to come out of the shadows. After a time, I decide to press on, telling myself that it was a crossed wire or other error. I continue to walk until I cannot bear to move, and then sit down on the damp earth of the forest floor.

The forest itself is a marvel, surviving by a process similar to photosynthesis, with the emissions from Myth's accretion disk serving as the source of energy. I place both of my hands onto the soil, and then curl my fingers into it, savoring the feeling of being anchored to something.

I do not make a fire tonight. I must conserve my strength for the final push tomorrow. Complete darkness covers me as Cinder turns away from Myth. My sensors alert me to alternative ways of seeing, but I allow myself to drift in the black. I curl my fingers more deeply into the earth and dare the Darkness to come.

"Come and take me," I say. "I'm ready, if it is my time."

The Darkness does not come, and I rest.

~

When the disc rises again, I marvel at the size of the Tower ahead. It is truly a magnificent architectural undertaking. It's a relic of a civilization that needed a purpose as the universe died in their skies, a monument to their own will. The Tower was meant to stand until the very end, defiant against time. They—we, I suppose—had beaten the odds so many times before that a final failure point had perplexed us. We'd been unable to cope with the idea that we may not be able to defeat death.

Every sentient organism knows on some level that it will die. Many minds can grasp and even learn to harness that knowledge. What those same minds then fail to grasp is that their work is also finite. All things, however grand, are mere fleeting ghosts in the face of the Darkness.

~

As I approach the Tower, I pass through the remnants of the city that once stood around its base. Most of it is now indistinguishable from the forest to the untrained eye, but I recognize the subtle rise of the ground where the Great Temple once stood. Huge white stone slabs still protrude from the vegetation. It's the place where I first arrived.

I remember, faintly, the faces of those around me when I opened my eyes for the first time. It seems insignificant now, even ridiculous, the grand elegance they bestowed upon the event. The temple was constructed for the sole purpose of receiving me, and allowing me to wake.

I remember color. It had been a vibrant world once. I opened my eyes before them, a manufactured being meant to proceed without them into the cold darkness of the future. So many flowers were hung from the walls that it looked like portions of the structure itself had been made from foliage. I sat on a similarly adorned throne, with a crown made from finely crafted glass and crystal.

They made me in their own image, not without a sense of irony, I suppose. Twelve Coda were awakened that day and asked to perform the simple task of continuing on.

They positioned us around twelve collapsed stars that would last succumb to the Darkness. For a time, I wandered among those that lived here, taller than they were and very clearly a manufactured being, but still enough like them that they had no trouble integrating me into their rituals and customs.

I did not serve any role in their government, but I came and went from their proceedings as I wished. I sat in vaulted rooms where decisions that affected the lives of millions were made, and I stood in dimly lit hospital rooms while decisions were made that would affect only one.

I watched all of them die, in time. After I laid the last of them to rest, I climbed the Tower for the first time. I mounted the first white stair and proceeded up, spiraling along the outside of the Tower, taking in the world below. The expanse of the now-vacant city stretched around the Tower, with lush green vegetation generously peppered within.

At the top of the Tower, I found messages waiting for me from another of the twelve Coda: Ash.

Their world's civilization had also ended, and they had climbed their own Tower in search of another voice. We were lucky to have been posted to two binary stars, orbiting one another at a distance of only 36 light-years. Although the messages I had from Ash were not verbose, merely reports from their system once every year, I still felt a great weight had been shared across the distance.

I stood atop the Tower for days, agonizing over the best way to respond. While my message would take over three decades to arrive, it would take me less than a minute to transmit.

I told myself that all great conversations, over time, begin with a greeting. I sent just one word, "Hello," and then descended the Tower.

I continued to receive the yearly dispatches from Ash, and I transmitted many more of my own in the time it took for my first message to span the 36-year distance.

At first I made sure to space my messages out, allowing Ash to receive them and not be overwhelmed. Eventually I realized that a flurry of messages wouldn't overwhelm me in the slightest. In fact, I waited impatiently every year for my single dispatch from Ash. So I began to send more messages, enjoying the outlet for my thoughts.

On the 36th anniversary of my first message, I waited at the top of my Tower as a cold rain fell, counting down the seconds. Nothing immediate would change, of course, but at that very moment I knew I'd been in contact with another being. I looked up, let the rain wash over my face, and I began counting the cycle again. Another 36 years for the reply from Ash.

A sound behind me stirs me from my memories, and I turn to investigate. Nothing. The sound had been close and sharp, as if someone had thrown a stone. My sensors detect nothing out of place, no movement.

I mount the first step of the Tower, noting how the pure white stone has become a faded grey with time, and begin my ascent to the top. It will take me most of the day to make the trip. The landscape around me, once lush and vibrant, stretches out in a murky haze.

As I begin to near the top, I feel one of my knee joints spasm wildly. I am just able to catch myself, and knock a stone from the crumbling stairway, sending it hurtling down to the ground. I realize what has happened. The sound I'd heard on the ground had come from the rock I'd just dislodged while keeping my balance on the stairs. Time has begun to slip more erratically than I'd calculated.

I manage to make it to the top of the Tower, though my knee has become increasingly unreliable. I will spend the rest of my time here, as I have few remaining spare parts for myself.

The top of the Tower is a circular courtyard ringed entirely by tall white pillars with no roof. The black sky hangs overhead, threatening to descend and engulf me. I look to the control stone in the center of the courtyard out of reflex and see the last message from Ash still hovering above it:

"Coda 11, final dispatch. All payloads delivered, final descent initiated. Goodbye, Cinder."

Seeing this message, cold and blue in the air above the stone, breaks loose a memory. I remember now. I'd read the message, then walked to the edge of the courtyard. I'd stood between two of the white pillars, looked to the point in the sky where Ash had been, and then I'd simply let myself fall. The impact must have damaged my memory, and left me in a daze. I reach to the back of my head and find a dent in the smooth metal plate there.

The last sentence in the message from Ash is against the code of conduct we had been instructed to follow for official dispatches, but there is no one to report to any longer. Anyway, I appreciate the sentiment.

Only Ash had called me Cinder. We weren't given names in the traditional sense, only our Coda numbers. When our numbers had begun to feel insufficient, we had taken the names of our stations as our own.

Both Ash and I received final dispatches from the other ten Coda Stations. They had come almost precisely in order, though five had outlasted six by two years. Like ten tones from a universal clock approaching midnight, they had come. Then it had been just Ash and I in a final grand duet.

Now I stand, alone on the stage with no audience, to face oblivion. I have my lines to deliver, and no one to deliver them to but myself.

I walk over to the control stone for the Coda 12 Station. I place my hand on the glassy black surface, and the display comes to life. There are no passwords or systems for verification, merely seven illuminated blue rectangles I am to push in sequence. I lay one finger down on the first. The stone is cold, and the blue rectangle disappears from the display.

The sound that comes, after so much silence, is cacophonous. A section of my planet-sized station decouples and tears away. The section on the far side of the planet begins its descent into the black hole below.

The matter added to the accretion disk stabilizes the space-time around Myth for a mere month, and the burning glow is magnificent as it fills the sky. For a while, there is enough light to see the forest again. I am struck by the range of color and brace myself against the control stone. I had forgotten how many colors there are.

After the month passes, I release two more sections, stabilizing the field for a week. I am ready this time, as brilliant light blankets the landscape once again. I sit between two of the white pillars, my legs hanging over the edge of the Tower. I try my best to catalogue every shade of color spread out below.

When I stand up a week later, I find that my damaged leg is completely unresponsive. I make my way back to the command stone slowly and deliberately.

When I decouple the last four sections, the Tower itself comes free from the planet-station and rotates to face Myth. This measure is taken in order to keep me as far within the stable field as possible. The last four sections of the station descend into the black hole below. Gravity is now negligible for the Tower, and I drift weightlessly as the last matter in the universe is spun into brilliant dust, and then consumed.

Soon, the Darkness will press in and overtake the fundamental forces of nature keeping Myth intact. How the scholars taught me to think about it is that Myth and the Darkness are approaching a point of equilibrium. Gravitational forces will be pulled apart, followed by the other forces down to the ones holding matter together. In the end, everything will become a smooth, horizonless space, devoid of ripple, echo, or light.

One of the more optimistic theories said that a flaw in the final merging of Myth and the Darkness will trigger a catastrophic release of energy that will push back the Darkness and begin another universe from the ashes of our own. It's evident, in the naming of the stations, which theory had gained more social approval. Perhaps my Tower will serve as the small piece of grit that causes some unforeseen divergence from the mathematical models.

My place, at the end of all things, is to strike the final note in the grand symphony of existence. It's a sentimental notion, but anyway it's one that's lasted.

As the accretion disc continues to dim, I turn and drift back to the control stone in the center of the courtyard. I wave my hand, dismissing the message from Ash. I place my hand on the center of the stone and it illuminates bright blue. This, the last light, will allow me to send one final dispatch into the Darkness. My message is predetermined, and I type it out carefully:

"Coda 12, final dispatch. All payloads delivered, final descent initiated."

I pause for a moment as the screen glows, awaiting my command. The blue light pulses, as the accretion disc above fades and then disappears completely. The light before me is now all that remains of us. Every breath, thought, and choice has led us here. I blink, and am momentarily terrified that the Darkness has finally come. My eyes flash open, and the blue light is still there. A fear of dying is not something I expected, but I suppose it is only right.

I reach out and type an additional line:

"Goodbye."

Because every great conversation, in time, ends with a farewell.

Daniel James Clark attended college at the University of Nevada, Reno, where he received a Bachelor of Arts Degree with an emphasis in photography, and a minor in journalism. He lives in Henderson, Nevada, with his family where he spends his time as a homemaker, photographing news events, maintaining a nonprofit website, and writing stories. @danjclarkphoto

the night shift

by Miriam Gauntlett

what can possibly save you now?
asks the night, bending
low over the derelict sprawl
of the inner city. the stars
look on with their faint
cold eyes and can't answer,
nor can the pulsing neon lights,
offering oblivion as the cure.
only the drum of people's footsteps
going home in the dark,
beginning to step in time,
provide a glimpse of hope. look:
there's a red sun on the horizon,
and it is dawning, dawning brighter
every day.

Miriam Gauntlett studies, works & writes in London. Her interests include revolutionary documentaries, long walks & tweeting @miriaaaaamg.

To a Child Who Does Not Yet Exist

by Kirsten Reneau

BY THE TIME YOU COULD BE old enough to read this, it's likely that you will have already heard of *Stellaluna*, a children's book about a fruit bat meant to make the animal seem endearing rather than dangerous. It was a favorite of mine growing up, and should you ever exist, I'm sure that I will read it to you like my mother did for me. Maybe you will trace the pages of the book in wonder and search for bats in all the dark places you find—basements, woodsheds, caves that answer only in echoes when you call for the friends you hope to make.

Did you know bats are born into an act of trust? Typically, the smaller an animal is, the less time they spend pregnant. But despite only weighing around seventy grams, bats are pregnant for nearly as long as humans. For seven months they hold their young inside them, allow their bodies to grow large and swollen with life. At the end of the seventh month, mother bats give birth upside down to a child who is up to one third of their own weight.

Because they are born upside down, the first thing that a baby bat does is fall. Completely blind, they drop down to the world below before they have the chance to open their mouths to scream. The mother must move quickly; in one motion she must offer her child up to the world and open her wings to catch it, protect it from the earthly laws we are all

bound to. When this moment—this original trust-exercise—
is over, she then holds her newborn close to her body. It is a
silent promise of safety, that she will not let go without warning again.

I have never been needed like that before, the way a baby
needs so completely.

I have been considering your maybe future-existence today. Getting to a place where the possible-you is actually possible has not been easy. Right now, you, like the bat, exist in
a liminal space between this world and another, in maybe a
hundred of the thousands of possible futures that lay before
me. I am at a crossroads in life now; I am just starting to
make true and tough decisions about the future. Do I want
to get married? Do I want to live in a city, or move home to
the rural landscape of the mountains? Do I want children?
These questions become more urgent each day, and perhaps
because of that, I have been thinking of the possible-you
more often.

There is a reason people hate bats; they cannot understand the place they have in this world, cannot see the good-
ness of the creature through the darkness that surrounds
them. I have been in dark places in my life, hidden in caves
so deep that there was no light, tried to bury myself under
the cover of night. I was so sad I thought it would kill me. It
was during one of those times, the almost-you, the *possibility*
of you, felt real.

You were not wanted. You were feared. I wasn't ready.

I had woken up on a mattress I didn't know with a man I
had never met before, my thighs stained red and ugly. I didn't
understand then, the wreckage that had been done to my
body. But I knew you represented a death, the end of life as I
knew it, if you could call the barely surviving that I was doing
a kind of living. For seven days, I bent over the edge of my

bed and prayed that you had not created your own genesis story in the darkness of my stomach, that you had not mistaken the broken rubble of my body for a cave of comforts, for a home you could live in.

On the seventh night, I drank three glasses of water before bed and slept with my arms wrapped tightly around my stomach, as if I could press you back into non-existence. The next morning, I squatted over a pregnancy test that, after a moment of panicked waiting, offered me a single stripe, crossing you out of the world. I felt relief, of course, but the possible-you had been born inside my mind, and you have lived and grown there ever since.

I am older now, old enough to tell you that should you come to exist, it is because I want you. I am at a place now where it is not a death, rather, a transformation of life. The lives where you exist and the ones where you don't no longer seem at odds with each other—just two different paths that only I can see, only I can choose. The future that you would come into is one where you have been chosen.

I worry, of course. I worry about the possibility of dropping you in a hundred different ways: that I will be a bad mother and leave terrible, unfixable scars across your psyche by virtue of my existence; that you may inherit the great sadness that has tried to consume me from the inside out; that you will have to leave me. The last one is inevitable. Even bats, who know that their mothers demonstrably saved them, still fly away sometime.

I try to imagine you, the physical you. Maybe you will be born completely bald, like I was. My mother, your grandmother, says that when I first came into this world she was convinced I was not her child. *Her eyes are so big*, she said, words slurred from the pain medicine. I imagine you like that, with large eyes, ready to experience all the wonders life has to offer. The possibility of it all is all so much that my heart feels ready to break out of my chest just thinking about it.

It is hard for me to consider the other half of the equation that would make you because in my imagination, you are so fully and completely mine. In Tonga, the bat is considered sacred, the physical manifestation of a separable soul. I know that should you become a reality, you will take a piece of me with you, a fragment of my soul snapped off and embedded into yours, so that you will always carry the innate, primal knowledge that I am learning to live with my arms spread wide, ready to catch you should you ever fall.

Kirsten Reneau is a writer from West Virginia. She received her MFA in creative nonfiction from the University of New Orleans, and her work has also been featured in *The Three-penny Review*, *Hobart*, *Hippocampus Magazine*, and others.

The Middle Ages

by Krishnakumar Sankaran

You will find your body is discrete:
your head, a tilted alembic. Your neck,
a funnel. Sometimes your voice will rise
like steam from furnace lungs to hiss nothings.
On coffee tables, your hands still as helpless birds.
They will flutter into air and sputter to a stop,
undecided. Some nights, your bones will lean weary
into your skin. You will learn to appreciate
their weight. Toes, squat pebbles.
You will see them settle into the ground and worry
sitting will root you. You will never sit alone.
You will learn to like the idea of not being an island.
You will find grooves where your face has learned
to set itself in a smile. You will find you smile a lot,
that there is little else to be done. You will find
you cannot remember how to look at the sky any more.

Krishnakumar Sankaran's work is published or is forth-coming in *CV2*, *Strange Horizons*, *Watch Your Head* anthology (Coach House, 2020), *Cha: An Asian Literary Journal*, and *nether*. He placed third in *CV2*'s 2021 2-Day Poetry Contest, and has been shortlisted for the Srinivas Rayaprol Poetry Prize in the past. He is based in Mississauga, Ontario.

The Tunnel: A Meditation on the Notion of the Future

by Brett Lyons

THERE IS A WAR BREWING, not within the world but ourselves. As we encounter the pains, disappointments, and melancholy of life, a common solution or, at times, a foundation for other solutions, is to live in the moment. Yet this becomes unobtainable so long as we continue to hold onto the notion of always needing to move forward. This is to say that the abstract concept of the future is a blockade of mindfulness. A possible solution to overcoming not only this particular siege, but suffering itself, can be explored through the idiom of the light at the end of the tunnel.

Life as Suffering

When Fredrich Nietzsche made that claim that "God is dead," he did so with a sense of humanistic optimism that it would lead to the elimination of an objective truth, thus allowing for greater understanding of the human condition. Yet if we take this declaration to be true, then the questions that arise become a horde of spectres that loom over our every moment. This is what existentialists would call angst; Albert Camus, The Absurd; and The Buddha, Dukkha or Suffering.

These questions come in many forms but hinge on Aristotle's elements of circumstance: who, what, when, where, and why. "Who am I? What ought I do? Why am I here?" These are examples of questions that plague humankind and cause suffering. By asking these, in essence, we are attempting to reconcile with our true nature, to transcend dualism and become monistic. Yet, it appears there is a cruel dichotomy between what we seek to know and what the world is willing to tell us. We know that this purgatory comes from the lucidity that allows us to comprehend the ephemeral nature of life. Both preceding and following life is freedom; but this particular freedom is not of concern so long as we accept that we cannot know what it entails. Instead, the only freedom that concerns us is the liberation that comes from overcoming the suffering of life itself.

Living in the Moment

To overcome this worldly suffering is the principle of mindfulness or living in the moment. It has become a proverb, the foundation of many forms of meditation, and the conclusion of many philosophies. Thus, the importance of it to those who see life as suffering is paramount, and in many ways it is simple; if life is so short, then valuing each fleeting moment is truly all we have. If suffering is carrying the weight of our desire to know in one hand and the silence of the world in the other, then this mindfulness is a peaceful body of water that calls us in to shed our weight. This would become a moment of pure relief and transcendence but is also a moment that seldom occurs, for this aforementioned water is hidden and the journey to find it is so perilous that at times our purgatory appears to be hell. Nonetheless, if any sort of reconciliation with our reality is possible, it must begin with the rectification of the mind.

The Levels of Delusion

Much of the human mind is founded on a hierarchy of delusions; things that prevent humans from seeing, or even attempting to see, the human condition and world for how it truly is. These delusions are what divide the mind.

Firstly, there is the delusion of material. This is when we flee from the weight of our condition by immersing ourselves in the material world of possessions, wealth, and other human bodies. This does not allow for any sort of introspection as the materially deluded person is too focused on the external world.

The second level of delusion is the realm of god. Once surpassing the material world, one is often tempted to indulge in a deity. This may come as a result of brushing paths with suffering and wanting to alleviate it as quickly as possible. These gods entail afterlives and in doing so, offer a quasi-peace since the believer is meant to trust in the god that their future will be good both in this life and the next. The danger of this delusion is that it cannot coexist with mindfulness. We cannot seize any moment if we forfeit our ownership of that moment out of hope that one day we will find peace. Especially when this hope is placed in the hands of a higher power, something that falls outside our realm of certainty. A god also relies on imposing a notion of the future in order for their followers to maintain their belief.

This notion of constant progression is the third delusion. Even the secular soul is deluded by humankind's abstractions. These are the fundamental concepts that give rise to our concept of self and by paradoxical nature, our understanding of the external. Even without believing in a god, we believe, consciously or not, that we are moving forward. This is the stage to overcome in order to truly live in the moment, but it is also the most difficult. Everything we do hinges on these ideas, specifically that of the future. All decisions, all pondering, all good or bad—what is good or bad—depend on the future, in some way or another, to exist. Yet by continuing to be deluded by this notion, we are still suffering.

An Internal War

Living in the moment has become a cliché of sorts, or at the very least, it is said in vain. We understand it is a solution, but we seldom act as though it is. The first and second levels of delusion can be overcome in many ways, but the third level is where the internal war begins and once begun, it stops in two ways: death or true peace. This division of the mind is not unlike an autoimmune disease. With an autoimmune disease, the body begins to attack itself, believing its own tissues to be wrong. In this case, the conscious mindset of living in the moment is battling the unconscious concepts that form the tissues which our understanding of the world is built on. And like war and autoimmune diseases, the outcome is suffering.

Even if someone is able to pull back the veil on the first two levels of delusion, the third veil is essentially invisible and thus the removal of it becomes unfathomable. This is why there is often a paradoxical effect when someone attempts to face and overcome the human condition. First, they understand that life is suffering, and second, they understand that they can overcome this by living in the moment. From here, they shift their mindset and attempt to abide by it. Yet, the result is often more suffering. This is because they continue to believe in the constant need to move forward which contrasts with their conscious mindset, resulting in the feeling of a protracted life. This is painful because if one sees life as short and attempts to appreciate each moment, when life suddenly feels gruesomely long, they are being undermined and betrayed. Thus, the light at the end of the tunnel continues to grow further and further away, so much so that they cannot even see it anymore.

The Tunnel

To truly live in the moment, the reconciliation of the mind is vital. With this, life becomes not long but how it naturally is, transient. This transience allows for the appreciation of the moment again. However, if this final delusion is the most elusive, then it may seem impossible to allow the mind to become one again. To navigate this, I call on the idiom previously alluded to, the light at the end of the tunnel.

As we enter this dark tunnel, we see the light at the end of it. This is simple enough; we ought to get to it. We enjoy our walk initially; however, as we move toward it, we notice the light growing further and further away as the tunnel grows darker and darker. Panic ensues as we frantically run to the light, but in such haste we fail to notice that the walls are closing in, and eventually we are trapped in the dark with only enough room to stand. If this tunnel is the purgatory we call life, the light is our notion of the future. Yet, if we understand that we must live in the moment but constantly move forward, then the suffering only increases as our internal battle grows bloodier; this is the contraction of the walls and our eventual entrapment. Ultimately, what seemed short has now become longer than ever imagined, and we are left with a simple question: what ought we do now?

I propose that we sit down in this dark tunnel. For if this tunnel is life, then the darkness is life in its purest form. The dark, like the nature of human, is awareness without ever truly knowing. We are lucid enough to understand that we will die, but we can know nothing else with certainty. At first, this is terrifying, but by sitting and meditating we can see that it is actually beautiful. For this dark tunnel is the condition that allows detachment from the final level of delusion. Without a light to push toward, we find ourselves in a moment that is neither long nor short. To enter this moment is to embrace the void, the unknowing, and the unruly path to the still body of water. In doing so, by the time you arrive at this pond, you will realize that your hands are now free of the straining weight you once carried.

This is bringing the mind together and finding the nature of human. This transformation can be illustrated with Yin and Yang; the dyad of disorder and order, suffering and freedom, dark and light. The tunnel is a moment of pure equanimity, or Yang, but if we are the battleground for a brutal war, then we are disorder among order just as Yin resides partly in Yang. However, by sitting down, closing our eyes, and entering the void, we become Yang within Yin or the light among the dark. This is how the tunnel becomes illuminated once again. Just as a sky lantern, we are encased by something physical but what produces light and keeps us afloat is internal. If we become the light, then we become free from suffering. In contrast, if we seek the light, then we are merely seeking freedom; this is looking to the future, a betrayal of the mind, and the perennial contributor to suffering.

This essay is dedicated to my Mother. Remember to embrace even life's most absurd moments.

Brett Lyons is an undergraduate student at Simon Fraser University. He is pursuing a major in English and a minor in philosophy. He hopes to obtain a Bachelor of Education so he can teach, as well as to complete a graduate program. He holds a particular interest in Camusian absurdism as well as Buddhist philosophy and hopes to continue to write about these philosophical schools with the possibility of writing a thesis centred around them one day. While he makes time for reading, writing, and teaching, more often than not he can be found in the abyss that is thought.

Future Perfect

by Diana Devlin

Will you stuff your capsule
with stories plucked from fading books,
the snug resonance of rhymes
old yet sure as Grandad's knee,
warm as the blood lines between you?

Smiles that soothe you
from the bathroom mirror,
the scent of lavender
puffing through your pillow
as you dream-drift
through future history?

Perhaps you'll pack it
with the patience of parents,
the strength of spider silk,
the tenderness of time's tick
by the sick bed
where memory presents
its sharpest point to write away
pain, pierce the skin of despair
and scribble on the sky
let the sun come back again.

Diana Devlin is a Scottish-Italian poet living and writing in Tuscany. Previously a translator, lexicographer and teacher, she has had many poems published online and in print, including a collaboration with a fellow poet which was published by Hedgehog Poetry Press in 2018.

When Spring Returns

by Olabisi Bello

IN DECEMBER, WHEN WINTER FIRST ARRIVED, it stormed the town with a brutal force that devoured every ounce of lush and green on the soil of Erlin city. The bubbling blue sky morphed into a cold slab of grey, void of any adornment from the vivid pink petals that used to stretch out from the branches of blossom trees. The once exuberant town was lifeless, cold, and empty. Romoke hated it so much that she cried. For half of the season, she sat on the brown couch beside the wall-to-ceiling window in her living room and watched as more leaves withered and fell to the snow-covered ground. No mellow holiday songs floated from the overhead speakers; no plethora of party invitations flooded her mailbox. The days had no choice but to trickle by and leave the joy of New Year's at Romoke's doorway. They also brought her sister with them.

It had started with a simple "knock, knock" then "knock, knock, knock" until her sister got inspired and broke out a whole album of beats right there at her front door. KNOCK—knock knock, knock knock. KNOCK—kn-knock knock, knock knock. For ten minutes straight. In the middle of the night.

"Romoke, open this door!" Wemimo called out and shook the door handle. "My fingers are turning red, biko."

Romoke shifted in her position on the couch, wrapped the quilt tighter around her body, and rubbed her forehead to soothe the piercing ache spurred by the irritating knocks.

"Leave me alone, Wemi."

"Just open this door and let me see that you're physically okay. We haven't seen you for a whole month. This is childish, sis. Haba please."

Romoke refused to open the door, no matter how many times Wemimo pounded the door or how many days she swung by afterwards. All alone in the house, her only duties were to eat, sleep, and take a shower at least once every two weeks. Nothing else moved her from that couch. She had stocked up on food and household supplies, so there was no need to leave. Not even the worry about her child, who she had dumped at her sister's place, or his likely resentment for her, stirred her from her lying position.

~

When March rolled around, the ice began to fizzle to steam, and the sun shook off slumber's cloak to pour its glorious rays on the sleepy town. Romoke knew she had to walk out of her frigid, dark home to the bright, outside world where the birds flapped across the sky, doling out melodious chirps, where the air was alive with the scent of daffodils, and tulips, and hyacinths along with that earthy aroma of soil mixed with the promise of rain. It was March 20, 2019, three long months after the accident. She had promised her sister via text that she would come back to the bakery when spring returned, so long as Wemimo didn't drop by to see her. But spring *had* returned, and Romoke wasn't ready to see it. So she gave in to her fear and plopped back on her couch.

The next week, once the nausea and the fears and the whispers had lessened, Romoke stepped on Irving Street, red bag across her shoulder, pantsuit pressed to a tee. Outside, it looked like winter never happened. The street was bare of any snow or ice, and the sidewalk was packed with strangers from different walks of life who kept brushing against her in their hurry to get to their daily jobs and earn that sweet bread. When she'd moved here fifteen years ago to start a family, the town had been a simple, quiet space where she could roam the streets for hours and barely come across two people, but now with the rampant suburbanization movement, everyone wanted a little piece of Glock County: the groomed man who strutted down the street as if he were the one that owned it, briefcase in hand, phone to ear, spittle flying everywhere; the disheveled mother who hustled her two children across the zebra crossing towards the school bus stop, brushing her hands against their unruly hair and struggling to fix hers. Everyone had somewhere to race to, a rush that mattered to them, but Romoke simply walked.

As she climbed the steps of the bus which arrived at the stop the same time she did, Romoke smoothed out her jet-black hair that had lost its waviness in the face of the tumultuous wind outside. The bus was as crowded as the path she had just left, with people stuffed into tiny seats and hanging onto poles.

"In or out?" the driver called out to her. She had stood on top of the steps for longer than she thought, watching the passengers like a weird creep. Some of them even gave her "bad eye" when she fished out coins from her bag and slipped them into the coin machine. The doors closed behind her, and she had to dig her shoes into the floor to stop herself from tumbling over as the vehicle jerked to life. She swore she heard sniggers. It would have been easier to walk to the bakery, and definitely less humiliating, but she didn't trust herself to walk down the same road she used to cross with Ibidun.

"Mummy, what's wrong with her face?" a little boy seated in front whispered loud enough for Romoke to hear, in fact, loud enough for the people around him to hear. They all lowered their eyes to the ground to hide their discomfort at the blatant, awkward question the innocent kid had just launched. Or maybe to cover their guilt at having stared at her as well.

The mother, comfortably oblivious, had her ears plugged by a set of headphones, watching something apparently funny on her phone. Romoke turned to the opposite direction and hoped that the boy would not repeat the question now that she was out of his direct line of sight.

"Mummy?"

Terror sunk in her like a boat anchor touching the seabed.

In a louder voice that drew the attention of more than a handful of people, the boy repeated the question.

"What, Brian?" the mother asked as she removed the headphones and placed them on her skirt. Romoke tugged the bell pull—hard—and rushed to the front of the bus, waiting for the doors to open at the next stop.

"I said, what's wrong with her face?" he whined. She shouldn't have taken the bus. She shouldn't have taken the bus. She should *not* have taken the bus. Funny how a solemn, heart-ripping walk to the bakery would have been less painful than being stuck on a bus with a boy who didn't know when or how to shut up. Romoke's arms began to shake and her fingers kept slipping off her bag, leaving sweat droplets behind. The rest of the passengers stopped whatever they were doing and shamelessly, *shamelessly*, observed the exchange.

"Whose face?" the mother asked in a confused but low voice as if trying to encourage the boy to lower his.

"Her!" He pointed his stubby white finger at the trembling Romoke whose teary gaze was fixed on the glass in front of her. The mother lifted her head to trace who exactly he was referring to, and then the doors opened. Romoke leaped out of the bus and balanced her feet on the concrete pavement. Without looking back, she ran down the street with an impressive speed for someone in six-inch heels. However, her peripheral vision had not spared her the image of the mother covering her mouth in shock. You see, when you wear your pain with a brave face, the world takes it as an invitation to poke and pull at it until you are left with nothing but hurt. And that boy had practically yanked out the shred of dignity she had just managed to restore. When she rounded an alley two blocks away from the bakery, Romoke backed into the wall behind her and let out the breath that had been stuck in her throat. She clenched her fists. Then unclenched. And re-clenched. Anything to stop herself from crying. She had done a whole mantra in front of the mirror before leaving and she had no plans on going back on it. *Do not cry. Do not be pathetic. Ibidun wouldn't have wanted that.*

In five minutes, she was in front of the bakery, her face as still as an unperturbed lake. The bell rang as she stepped into the little shop, welcomed by the smell of fresh bread and a mix of sweet, mouth-watering aromas. There were two customers, male and female, sitting by the window, giggling and laughing as they shared a piece of chocolate pound cake. The other red leather seats were spotless and empty. Romoke crossed the checkered tiles and walked up to the counter display in front where a blond clerk in a red apron was busy typing away at her phone. On noticing someone approaching, she tucked it away and put on a wide-toothed smile as she said, "Welcome to Romoke's Bakery. I'm Sharon. How may I help you?"

That stung. Ooo, that really hit home. She had built her store from scratch with her bare hands, and now she had to identify herself in front of a clerk *she* had hired.

"It's me. Romoke." Her eyebrow twitched. "The owner."

The clerk's eyes spread wide open until her eyebrows crossed half of her big forehead.

"Oh I'm so sorry, ma'am. Welcome ma'am. Would you like a seat, ma'am? I'm so sorry. I should have known it was you. I mean your pictures are everywhere on the store website, you know before the…" She shook her head. "Anyway, how is your day going? Do you want anything? Need anything?"

"Enough, Sharon." Romoke put her hand in the air and said, "Just get me the key to the office so I can get up to speed with everything."

"Oh, okay." She brought out a bundle of keys all linked to one huge key holder and slipped out two keys from the bunch.

"Here you go." She put them on the wooden counter. Romoke collected them and thanked her after which she made a move to walk around the display of confectioneries.

"You know, ma'am," Sharon toyed with the rest of the keys, "when I heard about the car accident and what had happened to your husband, I was so horrified that it had happened. I'm incredibly sorry for your loss."

Romoke flashed her a tight smile and walked into the office, leaving the door open to keep an eye on the shop. People weren't meant to bring up the accident. Her therapist had told her to let everyone she knew know that it was never to be brought up in front of her, but she had forgotten to brief the incompetent clerk that she had only hired a week before it happened.

The space looked exactly as she had left it, except it was much warmer than she remembered. There was no dust on any of the surfaces, and the window pane shone in the sunlight. Her sister had been doing a great job of taking care of the bakery and, hopefully, Tolulope, Romoke's child. She hadn't decided if she was ready to see him again. For three months, she had stayed away from him, cooped up at home, tortured by the reality that she was the one holding the steering wheel when the truck ran past the red light and slammed into Ibidun's side of the car. And she was the only one still alive. How was she meant to tell her own son that his father's blood was smeared on her hands?

A light tap on the door and Romoke looked away from her window to Sharon, who was fiddling with her apron.

"Someone needs to be at the counter, Sharon," Romoke said and sat on the big chair behind the desk.

"Oh, I'm sorry." She looked back at the shop to make sure no one had come in. "There isn't anyone here. The couple just left."

"Okay, so what is it that you want?"

"Umm I just wanted to apologize for saying I was incredibly sorry. It shouldn't be an incredulous sorry. It should just be a sorry. I'm sorry. I'm sorry for your loss, Mrs. Romoke."

Romoke shrugged. "You have nothing to be sorry for. You weren't the one that wasn't fast enough to avoid a truck large enough to have been seen from miles away."

Sharon walked up to the desk and placed her hand on it. "It wasn't your fault, ma'am. You know that, right? You couldn't—"

"I would rather not talk about this. Especially not with you. I have a therapist and we're working things out on the phone, and I believe he would do a much better job than a clerk who can't even manage to do *her* job properly."

Romoke closed the stack of files she was flipping through. She didn't need to glance at Sharon and see her downcast face to know she was being harsh. But she wanted to be left alone and that was her only priority.

"If you don't mind, I would like you to get back to the counter. Thank you."

"But—"

"Sharon. Leave."

The young lady sighed and retreated to the door.

"It wasn't your fault."

"Tell that to my dead husband. Please shut the door behind you."

Sharon walked out and closed the door, after which Romoke pulled out the bottle of antidepressants from her bag on the desk. She reclined back into her chair and rolled the tiny orange bottle in between her fingers. The doctor had prescribed one a day ever since she left the hospital, and she took it at night when the smell of blood and smoke stalked her and all she could hear was the squeal of brakes. It wasn't her fault. Everyone had said that. However, she had omitted significant details from her narration of the incident, details she planned to take to her grave. When they found the burnt car with Ibidun's scorched body still stuck inside, and her unconscious on the ground a couple of feet away, she hadn't gotten there by a miraculous slam that had propelled her so far away from the vehicle. She was awake after the crash had happened, completely disoriented and scarred, but conscious enough to unbuckle her seatbelt and run away. Her brain wasn't functioning properly—she had always suffered from short-term memory loss—so her fight-or-flight instinct was the one hastening her weary steps towards safety. It wasn't until she smelled smoke that she turned back to see that what had started as a small fire had now engulfed their entire car. Then she remembered Ibidun had been in the car with her. His screams from the backseat had jolted her memory.

Romoke popped the white pill in her mouth and followed it with a gulp of water from the dispenser to stop the bile rising in her throat. From her position on the desk, she could see a dying tree outside her window. She and Ibidun used to have little picnics underneath that tree during her lunch breaks. The once glorious blossom had now lost all of its petals to winter and looked like the arthritic arm of an old woman. It was March, the month of spring, yet the tree, like many others she had seen on her way, had refused to come back to life. Some of its branches had broken off leaving jagged pieces behind. It looked so sad yet so beautiful.

"It's the circle of life," Romoke sang in a whisper, then chuckled, knowing that's what Ibidun would say if he were here. She closed her eyes and relaxed into the seat, knowing that her nap wouldn't last long, and not caring if Sharon would rush in to ask intrusive questions when she would wake up screaming in the next fifteen minutes. She was tired. Exhausted to be honest. Maybe like the tree outside, she would never get revived and would have to live out the rest of her days as a lifeless being before being yanked from this earth. Nothing moved her anymore, not the smell of the bakery, or the color of spring, or the image in her mind's eye of her child smiling at her. She simply craved her husband, his burly arms wrapped around her shoulders, his firm but soothing voice telling her that without a doubt in his mind, he had forgiven her and that everything would be okay. But he was dead, and she just had metaphors that helped her find meaning in the little things, like Dr. Rashford had suggested. Winter for death. Spring for life.

She rolled her head over to look at the tree through squinted eyes. It was shriveled, but there could still be hope for it, and likewise her, that just couldn't be seen yet. Hundreds of tiny buds waiting to bloom into beautiful works of nature at just the right moment. Maybe, just maybe, she only had to wait.

Olabisi Aishat Bello is an aspiring biomedical engineer from Oyo State, Nigeria, currently studying chemical engineering at Howard University. Despite her passion for science, she has always loved the fluidity and joy writing grants, and she hopes to make an impact in society with this gift and her overall devotion to making the world a better place. She loves writing both poetry and fiction, and you can find her works in *trampset*, *Neurological Literary Magazine*, *Open Culture Collective*, and *African Writers*, among others. You can also follow her on Twitter @OlabisiBA.

Etymology

by Pasiphaë Dreams

I want a grandmother's name
lovely with vowels
like flowers in resin
        -elle or -ette?

I make a list,
        and listen
for the quiet percussion
of   -la   -el   -ie.
is that beautiful?

like a brooch made
for   -is   -sa   -se
pinned to her peacoat
        on the lapel,
owned by
        -lope, -lie, -lo.

I will be remembered
for how I whistle
-dette   -lene
between the teeth.

I control where we go
        from the palette
to our throat.
on the train, -aine
-leigh   -lynn.

see me then,
at a second glance.
another name, perhaps.

Pasiphaë Dreams @dreamofpasiphae is the alias of an imposter poet with many pronouns. As an emerging trans artist, he uses speculative fiction and poetry to explore gender and trauma.

Moment of Embarking

by Chitra Gopalakrishnan

IN THE HALF-LIGHT OF DAWN IN SEPTEMBER, the river Narmada glides tranquilly through the ancient riverine town of Maheshwar, cinnamon-colored at its furthest outstretch, a burnished copper in the middle, and a hazy orange nearer towards the bank where I stand, radiant and incandescent at the same time as she absorbs and reflects the light of the rising sun.

Moist breezes play subdued music in my ears in this quaint, speckless temple town in Khargone district in the state of Madhya Pradesh, in central India. Their clean breath, lush with the cool of a tapering monsoon and with the aromas of the damp earth, sal tree-sap, and dew-bright grass, leave the taste of Narmada on my lips, on my tongue, even as they lull me into a state of cozy childhood lullabies.

Even in my blurry state, I am alive to how these refreshing drafts are a reprieve from the everyday furnace in the northern part of India, from the quicksilver heat in New Delhi from where I have travelled, where the heat switches from dry to sweaty and steaming in minutes during this time of year.

Other aspects of distance, historical and cultural, play on my mind. I am aware that the flow of the river Narmada is through several time strata and there is no easy telling of the difference. The ninety-one, sepia-colored sandstone temples of Maheshwar, its several brawny forts bristling with ramparts and palaces crowned with cenotaphs, all of whom wrap themselves around the curve of the river with a purposeful elegance of style, give me a feeling of having traversed through centuries yet also of being comfortable in its clean and serene contemporaneity, in its current living and breathing spaces in the year 2017.

Swaddled by the hush of the present, the muted overhang of the past, the soft sibilants of the Narmada, the assured silence of the rising sun, the ever-so gentle melodies of the air and whiffs of earth-scents, the rising scale of birdsong jars. My being rebels at the petulant clamour of these feathered creatures that sound ignorant, misplaced, and somehow discourteous.

I wait to wind down my heartbeats and breath, to regain the space of silence, its power, not with my ears but my spirit, till I can once again hear the subtle. This blankness I come to is not an absence of life's cadences but their elevation, quite like hearing the wind in a cave, where sound and soundlessness merge, a state that brings me to the fringe of a meditative state though my eyes are open and I stand.

My attention wanders to the sun, poised and blooming into power from the edge of the world into the horizon. The extravaganza of this cadmium-colored ball is a show of how the sun suffices itself, of how it revels in its singularity. As its arc rises bit by bit in suspenseful radiance and as it anchors its way into the centre of nature's composition, I marvel at how its iconography, its heraldic vision—one that stands for wholeness, continuity, and infinity—gains surety within my consciousness, its tread noiseless, much like the sun.

I stand rooted, my attention sedulous, to take in the next stage of the sun's journey, its necessary travel, one that will bring about its complete dissolution and an end to dawn with finality. "The morning sight of this disc's melt-away at Maheshwar is as beguiling as its coming together in its wholeness," promise travelogues and yoga practitioners, who come here for sun salutations, alike. I see the sun give way from its centre by degrees, dissipate from a deep orange to sepia, from tawny amber to dull tan, till it disembodies into the Narmada in a liquid light, into a glassy transparency like a semi-molten mirror.

At the same time, my eyes are drawn to the waters of Narmada that chase the wavering color contours of the sun. I see how its waters' iridescence alters with a chameleon-quick swiftness only to settle into the ghostly shimmer of the sun, its shade of glossy pallor. A signal that the quiescent moments of dawn are up. A sign that says it's time for the frenetic routines of the day.

A craggy, loin-clothed, closed-eyed sadhu silently serenades the cosmos, waist-deep and one-legged in her waters, his other leg folded on his knee, blind to everything immediately around him. An image of my own guru who has brought me to these harmonies, away from the restless elements of the city, its unstill, on-the-move elements, attaches itself into my consciousness.

Not quite willing to forgo these enthralling moments, I sit down at the ghats, within the cool confines of one side of the populated, relict bank, from where I can see across to the other bank, speckled with rows of swaying and bright-tipped sal trees no longer suffused by the velvet veil of the pre-dawn hours.

The Narmada ribbons between us, in full swing, flushed with life. Remnants of last evening's offerings, delicate white jasmines nestled within handmade leaf cups and long, loose strands of strung marigold, bob up and down alongside small boats that churn its silky pale silver currents with their wooden paddles and return their passengers and devotees to the same raised position on its wave crests every three seconds.

As the cool light breezes continue to waver teasingly over my skin and billow around my person, making my loose cotton pants flap, I run my fingers through Narmada's brimming waters and wonder if I should indulge in a ritualistic dip for her symbolic power to come alive within. First immerse myself completely in her waters, then pirouette with my hands raised, follow this gesture by making a cup of my palms to drink a mouthful of her water, and then in an expanded, final gesture pour some of her water over my head in salutation chanting "Har Har Narmade" (glory be to Narmada).

A closer inspection of Narmada's impish wavelets that eddy, curl, and vanish into her flinty depths, however, offer a warning against impulsively losing myself in the sanctity of the river. The cautionary words of a cheerfully dissolute pundit hollered yesterday, a little past noon when Narmada's waters are blue-green, echo.

I can almost see and hear him now in his satiny saffron-silk kurta, his thick gold chains, his hirsute arms, his face full of flesh folds, his tongue devil-red, and his sentences gushing out of a mouth thick with the slushy remains of betel leaves. "Don't be deceived by Narmada's mildness. Beneath her glistening surface are currents whose undertow is swift, strong, wild, and vicious," he bellows. "You don't want to die, do you, with your inexperience in the water?" He reminds me of a gargoyle that spouts water and wisdom in the same breath.

Even as the temple bells above the ghats peal, the brass plates pound, the songs of devotion by the pundits reach their pitch, and the crescendo of the morning aarti arrives, where lights with wicks soaked in ghee are lit and offered first to the deity and then its smoky flames are passed around to the devotees, I remain in this state of capture, in a private and personal world, where all anxious rational thoughts of my neural circuits are obliterated, my mind emptied and my spirit in a place of its own.

This is what I have come to Maheshwar for. To allow my mind to settle. To allow myself to disentangle from daily involvements of city life. To give myself the permission to stand undisturbed. To let go of all the glues of my tangible world. To flow into meditation naturally.

I go back to my guesthouse for now but come back every day in the small hours before dawn…for five months…for these very same sights. Of my trysts, Ram Dayal, my portly, moon-faced, genial, and well-read guesthouse manager, observes in chaste Hindi, "I think you tirelessly lope down Narmada's banks every day to test your level of calm. And I think, you also strip your inner self each time to see if your balance is chancy or you can sustain it within and without." His tone is one of wry amusement, but I cannot deny its deadly accuracy.

My sense of equipoise at Maheshwar is both visceral and intangible.

I try to explain my feelings about this contemplative morning mood of Narmada, her effect on me, of how the geography of Maheshwar has imprinted itself on my fifty-five-year-old mind to my guru, Ravi Shankar. He likes to be called thus. Minus the title of guru.

He is helping me find what I seek.

My guru of eight years is a tall man with a lean frame, an easy manner, a sanguine, unlined, and youthful face, though he is in his seventies. His faultlessly white kurta and lean pants and white close-cropped hair define him in the way clouds define rain.

He came into my life when many of the things failed to make sense and I had reached an end of sorts. Worldliness brought a sense of dismay, work felt like an unintelligent, unrewarding board game, prayer distracting rather than transporting, and the closing of my eyes fetched emptiness rather than relief. I was looking for something more, a different frame of faith.

Even before I met him and accepted him as my guru, his disciples described him to me as a man of few words. Leela Madan, who has been under his tutelage for fifteen years, every so often, tells me of how he can "go back in loops of time and cracks in space" and "read people and their problems like a written page." It prepares me for his reading of my life with accuracy, though I have not been explicit. The prescience in his eyes is a giveaway of his knowingness.

Guru Ravi Shankar offers me a route to know myself. Seeing my own truth, before I try salvation or to know the world. His way is a compelling one. A start with the sharpening of my sensibilities and cultivating my self-knowledge in order to understand the workings of the universal.

"It is a way guided by Hindu philosophy and practitioners over millennia," he explains. "One that is not based on Hindu religion with 36 million divinities. Nor on tradition, or dogma, or faith or orthodoxy, but in something deeper. Something that involves filtering out the chatter and learning the sound of your own voice. This route will take you on your own journey, one that will be uniquely yours, unlike that of others, even if they set out with you at the same time and at the same place."

Said in his voice and in his manner it sounds disarmingly simple, though I know it is far from that. I trust him completely.

I have trusted him ever since I felt his energy when he extended his right hand over my head to bless me. Wildly illogical, unreasonable, unbelievable? Not for me.

I talk to him about Narmada, hesitant and nervous of appearing like a naïve, mad celebrant. "Narmada's muted undertones, her fluid serenity at dawn have unloosed me, layer by layer, over these months, tenderly and with caution first and then with more flamboyance. Her waters urge me to feel and see myself as I have never done before. She mirrors the trueness within me, washes away my lifelong anxieties of being fractured and frustrated, fearful and alone, and shows me that I have an enough-ness of spirit to live fully in the world. She also shows me that my broken psyche can be made whole again by seeking a larger purpose. Despite seven years of tenacious effort, inner rigour, and yogic practices to regulate life forces in the city, I have been unable to arrive at this state of equilibrium, a state where I feel happy wheels of energy within my abdomen. So I know I will forever carry a drop of Narmada within me just as every grain of wheat and rice in this region does."

To my breathless gust of words, at first, he simply says, "I think you will now understand why so many saints and all manner of people have said the mere act of contemplating the Narmada can absolve you."

Then as an afterthought, he adds, "Narmada is placid at this time of the year in Maheshwar. But not always. And even as she flows through this state, from her headwaters in Amarkantak, through Mandla, Hoshangabad, and Nimawar, and then downstream to Karanjia and Patan, she changes her moods and colors capriciously. As an angry torrent, she is Rewa, in restfulness she is Manananda, bringer of eternal joy, where she is spirited she is called Rajani, as a seductress, she is Kamala, and in places where she destroys she is Vibhathsa. She is similarly called by other names in the two other states she flows in, Maharashtra and Gujarat."

I am keen to talk about Maheshwar as it is he who has suggested I come here to "cut away from all social and emotional connections to see life from inside out." I pause, uncertain, to see if he will let me. He nods with a smile so I continue, "The town of Maheshwar with her clay houses, ochre-tiled roofs and low brick walls, with her wrinkled fields of cotton, wheat, and soybean, with the click and hum of her villages, and with her people's quiet community involvement on the one hand, and with her classic, symmetrical historical structures of religion and ruling on the other, somehow pulls in her many facets into a harmony of being. This truth of Maheshwar, her innate integrity has shifted something within."

I wonder if my interspersing of the cartography of an outer world into an internal world is simplistic, banal, the work of a neophyte. Fortunately for me, my guru comes up with a delightful surprise. He saves my observations from the humdrum and shows me fun in the fuzzy spaces between philosophy and spirituality.

With a wicked glint in his eye, at least it appears thus to me, he says, "Maheshwar is Lord Shiva's town, the Destroyer in the Hindu trinity. He balances the power of the Creator Brahma and the Preserver Vishnu, to destroy all things negative, be it evil or ignorance. He delivers things he destroys to Brahma when they are ready for recreation. Yet believe me when I say he has some unhallowed passions and not all of the town is sanctified. Do you know Nandi, the sculpted bronze bull, who is Lord Shiva's guardian at the temple above the ghats, jumps his cage and takes on the form of a fierce, black bull, and cavorts around town? And that the size of Lord Shiva's idol grows by the size of a sesame seed every year?" I am amused by the bull's devilish sense of humour, his crooked, uninhibited internal transformations, as I am glad for the liveliness within Maheshwar at the bit of personal strangeness of Lord Shiva's idol.

In the month of February in 2018, when the chill webs Maheshwar, I feel a certain inexplicable readiness towards many things. I sense I am at the right point of my personal evolution and that my moment of embarking has arrived. Not so much through external signals as an inner knowing. I confide in Leela when I feel my shift from traditional frameworks of cognition.

"Are you ready to let go of the world of appearances, the temporal world of reality? To trust in the power superior to the intellect? To transcend sense-experience and go to a place unverifiable by science, one beyond the Western empiricism that you are familiar with, and handle the polarity of this space? Are you prepared to trust in the metaphysical base of the philosophy of Hinduism that will connect your being, your finite atman, to the universal brahman, the ultimate invisible reality that encompasses everything, even Gods, in a unity?" she volleys unceasingly but not caustically.

Her intent is probably to assess my capacity to cast away my many familiarities and to shoulder the implausible complications these experiences will bring. My potential to withstand instances that will be qualitatively different from anything I have seen or known so far.

My guru has talked to us over the years of this inner journey. "Your inner journey, darsana, or the soul-sight as we call it, will not ascertain and acquire facts, or illuminate truths of revealed religion, but will take you on an unfamiliar, expansive quest of values, one that will align you with the true nature of reality as it begins to gradually reveal itself to you."

He speaks of this as being each one's subjective journey, distinctly one's own with no roadmaps to follow. In his words, "It will be your direct and intimate knowledge of the reality of truth, its élan vital, or its vital impulse. You have to make your own inner way, and, at the beginning, it may not be necessarily comforting. Foot sores rarely are."

Rajat Sen, my ex-colleague and friend, seeped in city life, discredits, in a phone call from Delhi, my efforts at "creative intelligence, my intuitive inner search for ideal values through my innate sense of knowing." He pooh-poohs it abrasively as "so much nonsense" and commands me back to New Delhi.

"Dissecting your experiences within your head as a template for God's attributes or universal intentions and matrix is plain stupid," he snaps. After an awkward pause between us, he says in a less ill-natured tone, more as an appeal to my sanity, "It is without any logical support, has no methodology which is measurable and demonstrable or recognisable sources of knowledge."

I know many in my family and friend circles are variously alarmed and puzzled by my contrarieties over the years, their stares of incomprehension say it. Fortunately, my husband's happy indulgences of my exploits save me from hostility within my innermost circles and also from dealing with his internalised angst. And as I am not interested in co-relating my explorations with the bells and whistles of calculations or technology or counter-defenses, I let Rajat keep his faith in knowledge, using empiricism and rationalism in its exactitudes, as I go on an undefined exploration.

I know drifts of knowledge gained through intuitive powers require preparation and can be trusted only if the seeker is well equipped to handle its inner truth. My first brush with such intuitiveness comes as I quiet the turmoil within and I am in balance with my surrounding elements of earth, water, fire, air, and space.

~

I sit on the banks of Narmada. It is the hour of the Creator within the trinity, the Brahma Muhurtha, at 3:30 am, when everything in the universe is said to be in its perfect state. My diary, dated February 3, 2019, where I ink my thoughts, best conveys my first experience, my initial, small epiphany: "I am in a space where the play of my senses dull and my conscious thoughts subdue. With no sensory stimulus to delineate the borderline between the self and the world, I arrive at a space where I am endless and intimately interwoven with everyone and everything. My sense of self diminishes. I find myself naturally involved in a vaster existence yet one which is one with my own. I know it sounds contradictory and abstruse, more so when I say I make sense of these things in an impersonal yet deeply personal way."

Yet I cannot think my intuitiveness away or disbelieve it in any way, however maddeningly opaque or insane it sounds to others. And what is remarkable is that there is a simplicity to my knowledge even though it is so profound.

My next understanding, above the threshold of stimuli, comes to me after a month, with relative ease and felicity, almost in a just-like-that way. Of this I say in my writings: "Time has no meaning. Past, present, and future exist simultaneously. When time stops, all problems disappear. As endlessness prevails, I no longer identify with the body or the mind. And in this mellow state, the thought 'I am and I am aware' comes. As does the understanding of 'I am, I was, and always will be, beyond all worlds and all universes, infinite and beyond time.' From this, I know that death and the afterlife are just small incidents."

In my last entry on April 25, 2019, in a hasty summary of my inner scape, I write: "What can I say of this experience except that this luminous floating-ness is bliss? How can I try to utter that which is unutterable in mortal speech yet something that is true and exists? All I can say with certainty is that this primary consciousness functions with its own inner logic, where it is its own means of knowing, and that one can merely know by feeling it. And also that I have arrived at a higher definition to my person though my sense of self is diffused."

I know that my inheritances are small, infinitesimal, just at the very beginning, and the arrival of the supreme reality is a long way in coming, and in all likelihood will take more than one lifetime. But having had a glimpse of it, this is the world I want to be in as I am sure its difference will keep me enchanted for life.

~

I plan a move to Varanasi. Kashi as the locals call it, or Benares as my guru refers to it, which is further north in the state of Uttar Pradesh. I will move with all my co-disciples and my guru to yet another city of Lord Shiva, one of the oldest in the world and a centre of civilization for more than 3,000 years. The revered river Ganga flows through it, and to die in Varanasi, close to this river of purity, is to break free from the endless cycle of rebirth. The promise of Lord Shiva is immediate liberation.

I do not intend to go there for salvation or for whatever it is that the six million tourists will aspire to in their visit there this year. I will go instead to take on the challenge of finding my interiority within the greater depth of this city, where the cult of death is the same as the cult of life. Where the cremated dead from the Manikarnika ghat and the living worshippers at the Dashashwamedh ghat and the 87 other stone ghats walk the same paths.

Will I be able to do it?

My co-disciple Manish soothes my apprehensions of doubting in this manner with patience. "Doubt helps you shake the status quo, face and overcome your inner fears, rethink success as you see it, reflect on previous stories you've told yourself, ask yourself new questions, and search for new answers."

I am now able to accept doubt as an important part of my journey.

"Varanasi's macabre welter of sanctity and strength can frighten an initiate who uses the energy of the external place to forge a way inside. Lord Shiva's avatar here is not the gentle one in Maheshwar. In Varanasi, he explosively breaks social, moral, and legal codes and rebels against order," warns Veena. "Are you sure you are ready both for the city and to withstand the essence of Lord Shiva's vehemence that is not altogether sane?"

I am not sure, but I am ready to forgo the comforts of the familiar. With help from my guru.

Countless people have described the living crematorium drama that is Kashi.

I read the relentless details of their writings, in their multiplicity and variety. Of the sights of corpses lying on bamboo biers wrapped in white cloth waiting to be burnt, the endless stacks of pyre wood gathered haphazardly, the blazing fires from dawn past dusk at the ghats, the fire-aided decomposition of human flesh, the bodies of babies and holy men tied to flotsam and floated downriver, the riot of claws, talons, and beaks of predatory birds who fight each other to eat putrefying flesh, the unavoidable jostling with goats and cows who come to chew on the flower offerings for the dead, and the raucous chants of the pundits who combatively transact the business of death.

I also know that the river Ganga has been gutted in Varanasi beyond remedy by these activities, of how its murky water carries the ashes of 30,000 people cremated there each year, of how the faithful yet believe it is pure enough to drink.

It throws me in a spin.

Will the city's upturned, irrational, and absurd polyphonies catch me off-guard? Will its haphazard growth, where the flying brick dust of modernity has been awkwardly overlaid over traditions, throw me off my trail and unspool the small inner balances that I have just come to? Will the Ganga be my lifeline as the Narmada is?

Kashi, I know, will be a hard personal litmus test, a true assessment of whether I can keep my calm in its cacophony, and then as I resume my normal life in New Delhi.

Perhaps, for a fuller consideration of the city and its confusions, its whirling verbal and visual codes, I could make a start by listening to the city's multifocal narratives, grapple with their lyrical anxieties, as their subversive practices of using indirection as a storytelling strategy. Maybe then a blurring of the sounds of the conch, bells, chants, bargains, and howls will happen and allow me to hear the subtle sounds of my inner life.

Maybe, maybe, maybe. I shall lay my faith in my current belief that life has a way of leading me to exactly where I need to be and do exactly what I need to do.

First published in Libretto Magazine, *Issue 04, December 28, 2020.*

Chitra Gopalakrishnan, a New Delhi-based journalist and a social development communications consultant, uses her ardor for writing, wing to wing, to break firewalls between nonfiction and fiction, narratology and psychoanalysis, marginalia and manuscript and tree-ism and capitalism. chitragopalakrishnan.com

Sometime, in the future

by S. Rupsha Mitra

Gradually we could wrap ourselves in the arduous sheathing
comfort of the fog of oblivion, gradually we might
end up in this slow drifting into a barren land devoid this
    bewildering gush
The thrilling sensation of dopamine and adrenaline—
The exciting brain chemistry burbling into some sort of love.
Someday it might be like the drudgery of indefinite times, it
might be a transformation of the silk lacey lilac strings
bonding us, which suddenly waft into a separation, a
change of minds, eventually it could be that we
both forget each other at the same time, forget the
moments of our wintry shelters and mango summers,
wounded healings and all the twinkling shimmers of
glittering sheen of oblivious times.
So, do you think before we leap into such anonymity for
    any thing
between us, we must reach for the edge of bliss—an
unburdening fulfilling, crackle it in sunbath and rainfall,
with the floating glimpses of our unending dreams?

S. Rupsha Mitra is a writer from India with a penchant for everything creative. Her work has been published or is forthcoming in *opia*, *From the Farther trees*, *Ethel*, *North Dakota Quarterly*, and *Indian Literature Journal*.

Peter Cushing Rides a Bicycle

by Nadia Steven Rysing

For the Jellybottys, whose lyrics I have misremembered for over a decade.

PETER CUSHING RIDES A BICYCLE in the town that I am from. Not the actor who died in 1994, but the child born in 2017, conceived at an advance showing of *Rogue One* by two stoned lovers who believed in the power of CGI to bring the dead back to life.

Today is exactly twenty-two years from that date, though our Peter Cushing hasn't remembered anything about all that. Today our Peter Cushing is riding a bicycle that he was gifted from a friend because today is the day that Peter will ask his boyfriend to marry him. Peter lives in one city and he must get to the other city. There are only two cities on the base of the Saugeen (once Bruce) Peninsula: Nawash (once Owen Sound) and Zaagiing (once Port Elgin), but they are far apart and it is not safe to go on foot. So today Peter is riding a bicycle, a bright blue bicycle crafted just around the time that the Breakdown happened. It's in remarkably good shape. A good bicycle from Before is hard to come by, you know, but Ron finds them and fixes them up just right. But this one, this one is special, and the only one Ron gives to Peter on a day like today.

Peter goes to the gates of his city, and he listens to the watchers' recommendations for solo travel across the Peninsula. Look both ways. Ring your bell if you see wilderpeople (this usually scares them off) and signal with a flare if you need help. There's a stopping point at Allenford (make sure you take a break, it's 45 kilometers after all!) and there Peter can access iodine tablets if he's feeling a little off. Peter listens to all this and he agrees, but he is not really listening too closely. Today he is asking Nigel to marry him, after all, and there is very little else he can think about.

Peter doesn't have a ring to propose with. Nigel would lose it gardening like he loses everything nice, and he would be annoyed at Peter for giving him something else to lose. But Peter has a plan for this. Peter always has plans for everything.

Peter rides his bicycle most of the morning, only stopping when a herd of wilderpeople are crossing the road. They move slowly as their wranglers guide them along, back up north where they will be transferred to Manitoulin Island and kept out of trouble. One snaps its teeth at Peter, but the wrangler reprimands it kindly and Peter swears he can see the wilderperson look almost fondly at the wrangler. It gives Peter a little hope if he ever turns. He will not be himself if he does, of course, but he will still be treated with respect and dignity.

In Allenford, Peter stops to stretch his legs and eat his packed lunch of TVP with rice and a bit of soy sauce. He talks to a pair of travellers, these two on horseback. They are taking a tour of the Frontier. That is what people in the big cities call this area. It's been many years since the wilderpeople were escorted out of the other cities and many people still fear them. Peter remembers those times, he was young and impressionable after all, but he tells them of his encounter this morning and, after they smile, he wishes them well on the rest of their journey. He advises them as well that when they go north into Chippewas of Nawash Unceded First Nation to be respectful and check in with a watcher station as soon as possible so the watchers would know to look for them if they go missing. It is custom, Peter tells them, to thank the watchers with gifts of tobacco and reminds them that it is a privilege to be able to visit the area and not a right.

Neither really listens. Peter thinks to himself that he should visit his great-uncle. They could go up to Neyaashiinigmiing, where his great-uncle was born. That is where Peter lived during the worst of the Breakdown and he has many fond memories living there. It would be nice to go back home together. He met Nigel there two summers past, both volunteers restoring the old lighthouse. It was on that pebbled beach at sunset where they shared their first kiss.

After this break, Peter Cushing goes back onto his bicycle and continues down Highway 21 on his way to Zaagiing. He stops when he reaches a great field of wind turbines. He admires them for a time before he goes down to the flowers growing beneath the great blades. The long, hardy sunflowers grow in many places on this highway, cleansing the dirt of the poisons once used to target the wilderpeople. Sunflowers are Nigel's very favourite plant, and the gardener treats them as others once treated gold. Precious and valuable above all else.

Peter cuts a few stalks, gently and precisely as Nigel taught him, so he can obtain flowers without hurting the plant. He bundles these with the blue ribbon that Nigel's mother has given Peter as a token of her blessing. Peter puts this in his bicycle's basket and he returns to the road.

The soy fields outside Zaagiing are dormant, but still green even with the chill in the air. Peter goes to one farm, the closest to the highway, and he rides his way down a trail until he reaches the ancient homestead and the brightly painted mobile homes that line the lawn. He rings his bell excitedly outside the home Nigel shares with three others, and his beloved comes to the window to see who is there.

Nigel sees Peter and his face breaks into a grand smile. He knows Peter and he knows without words why Peter is here. His roommates watch not so subtly from the windows as Nigel comes out to the peony garden that he has grown in his leisure hours. Others from the commune peek out to see what is happening, but neither Nigel nor Peter notice. They only have eyes for each other.

Peter barely gets down on his knee before Nigel says yes. The neighbours applaud as Peter gets to his feet and sweeps Nigel into a deep, deep kiss.

They do not wait long to marry, and in a few short months our Peter Cushing becomes Peter Thompson. He does not keep his name, no, but he does keep the bicycle.

Nadia Steven Rysing (she/her) is a poet and speculative writer living on the Haldimand Tract in Southwestern Ontario. Her work has appeared in *Black Telephone Magazine* and under a previous name in "No Place For Us," *Spirit's Tincture, Wizards in Space, Eye to the Telescope,* and *Strange Constellations.* You can find her on Twitter @a_tendency.

ABOUT THE EDITOR

Angela Caravan is a settler on unceded Coast Salish territory (Vancouver, BC), and writes both poetry and fiction. She is the author of the micro-chapbook *Landing* (post ghost press). Her work has also appeared in *Broken Pencil*, *Pulp Literature*, *Cascadia Rising Review*, *Sad Mag*, and more. She is the publisher at Bell Press and also runs the Decameron Writing Series (decameronwritingseries.com). You can find her on Twitter at @a_caravan.